Golden Streak Series Book 6

KATHI S. BARTON

WCP

World Castle Publishing, LLC
Pensacola, Florida

Copyright © Kathi S. Barton 2015
Print ISBN: 9781629892078
eBook ISBN: 9781629892085
First Edition World Castle Publishing, LLC, January 30, 2015
http://www.worldcastlepublishing.com

Licensing Notes

Cover: Karen Fuller
Editor: Eric Johnston
Editor: Maxine Bringenberg

Chapter 1

Keith tried to get into the conversations around him, but he just couldn't seem to focus. He'd been working on the project that had come across his desk and hadn't wanted to go out on this date. He glanced at the woman on the seat next to him, and for the life of him he couldn't remember her name. Britney something, he thought, but he couldn't be sure. When she smiled at him, he grinned back.

"Did you have a good time?" He told her he had. "I'm glad you finally agreed to go out with me. Mia said that I should have asked you out long ago, but I'm not really like that. I like to be asked out. It's the way things should be."

"You're not like what?" Keith knew he didn't have a great deal of social skill, especially around women, but he really despised the games they could play when they felt you needed to guess their every thought. He wanted a woman to date like his sisters-in-law, where if you screwed up they let you know and when you asked them something, you'd better be prepared for the answer. But instead of answering him, she giggled.

He looked out the window at the passing trees. He frowned when he realized how fast they seemed to be going. Even if the roads had been plowed of snow there was no reason for them to be going this fast. He looked at his friend and asked him to have the driver slow down.

"Oh, don't be a spoil sport, Golden. You know as well as I do that we're perfectly safe in here. And you should feel doubly so. I don't think I've ever known anyone to wear their seatbelt in the back of a limo before." Laurence Whitney had been his friend since grade school, and it wasn't until lately that Keith realized he didn't have a clue why. "You should learn to live a little and enjoy life more. I plan to live the rest of my life to the fullest, like I'm never going to wake up tomorrow."

Keith decided that he simply wanted to live. He reached up to knock on the glass between them and the driver when he felt something bump the limo. He turned to look behind them, and lights that seemed to come from nowhere were coming at them very quickly. When the car was bumped again, he turned to tell Britney to buckle her belt, but a sickening crunch made him realize they'd been hit again, and this time the limo wasn't taking it so well. It slid all over the road, bumping into things as it did. When he felt the car lurch forward, he reached for the girl but she was gone. He looked at the woman Laurence had been kissing only moments ago, and her mouth seemed to be opened incredibly wide. He heard her screams, but when they stopped abruptly, he knew that on some level she was hurt very badly.

Broken glass was flying everywhere. He felt the seatbelt cut into his chest and hips and felt as if he were flying, and without the support he'd be on the ceiling of the limo like Laurence and his girlfriend seemed to be. Something tore at his face, glass he supposed. But when a pain in his chest seemed to take his breath away, he felt something hit them again.

Screams tore through the large area, and he watched in horror as Laurence flew through the window that had been between them and the driver. When he went through the windshield, Keith saw what was left of the driver as trees flew past them at a sickening speed. His head was missing, but his hands still held tightly to the steering wheel. Keith felt a laugh burble from his mouth when he wondered just for a second if he was pressing on the gas too.

Branches with snow in them slapped at the front seat. Glass and red paint seemed to color everything in a bright Pollock type of artwork. Trees, then snow, then trees again made him realize that the limo was rolling again. He had to close his eyes for a moment as the motion made him sick to his stomach. As he reached for the girl she screamed, and her soaking wet hand slipped from his when they came to a sudden and profound stop. He cried out in pain and passed out.

Warm sticky wetness covered his face as he tried to move. The engine was ticking, and he could hear someone still screaming. He had a thought it was him, but put his hand to his mouth and found it shut. He wondered if it was one of the others and thought he should help them. Moving his legs, he felt them trapped. He was pinned in the car and he was getting weaker.

He felt someone touch his mind, but he couldn't seem to connect, so he tried harder to concentrate on the voice.

Keith, tell me what happened. Are you hurt?

Ryland, he thought.

Keith, where are you? Tell me, buddy, so I can come to you.

I don't...we rolled and rolled. He felt something bubble from his mouth and put his hand there. *I'm bleeding, Ryland. I think I might die. I can't find the others. Laurence was here, but I think...he's dead. So is the driver.*

He tried to move again, but he hurt and cried out from the pain. When he looked down at his chest, he touched the large piece of glass that seemed to be a part of him. Touching it with his fingers, he screamed out in pain again and told his brother what he'd found.

Don't move. I'm coming. Tell me what you remember last.

Keith saw his friend laying a few feet in front of the limo, his body broken and staining the snow a deep red. He told his brother.

I think he's dead. He felt his brother's fear. *I'm cold, Ryland. And tired. I can't...I'm going to die.*

No you're not, damn it. Tell me where you are. He couldn't. Keith could no longer think, and felt himself fading faster. He could hear Ryland and his demands to stay with him, but he couldn't and closed his eyes. Christ, wearing his seat belt didn't save him at all. He looked up when he saw a face just coming into focus, and he smiled at her.

"Are you an angel?" She cursed at him. "I would think they'd frown on that." Keith closed his eyes and felt his cat cry out. He told him he was sorry but he couldn't shift for him right now. Then he felt the air leave his body as he slipped away.

~~~

Harley looked at the man with the glass in his chest through the busted window. The fucker was as good as dead and she knew it. Putting her hand on the door that was jammed up, she looked around before pouring her power into it and jerked it from the hinges. She reached in and felt his pulse. Still beating. She moved toward the front of the limo and her stomach jumped.

"Christ," she thought aloud. "Where the fuck is your head?" She moved around to the front of the huge car and found a dead man with a broken neck lying in the snow She looked up the hill to where she'd found the first of them and wondered if she'd suffered much. Her body had been run over by the big car, and by the looks of what was left of her she'd gone through the side window.

Harley was coming around to the other side of the car when she heard a cell phone ringing. She saw another woman when she pulled the other back door off, but it was the man with the glass dagger in his chest that seemed to be ringing. Harley reached in and touched his throat again.

She picked up the phone and, deciding it might be the only way to get someone to find their bodies, answered it.

"Yeah?" No one answered for several seconds, and she nearly put the phone down before the person finally spoke.

"Britney? Or is this Carly? Can you tell me if Keith is all right?" The man sounded desperate. "Please? I was just speaking to him and I lost the connection. I would really like to speak to him."

"I'm not either of them, but I can tell you that there has been a hell of an accident. There are four dead and one nearly. You tell me what this Keith person looks like and I'll tell you if he's the breather or not." She looked at the man who was still breathing. "He's not going to make it, I think. He's got a large piece of glass in his chest that's pretty much hit his lungs and maybe his heart."

"Fuck." She waited while he went through an impressive vocabulary of curse words and decided that she might use a couple of them. "He has dark long hair and blue eyes. He's twenty-seven and he has on a tux." She looked at the man in front of her. So far his description wasn't helping her.

"Buddy, in case you hadn't noticed, it's dark out. They all have dark hair. I don't know the fucking color of his eyes, but I can tell you that both men have on tuxes. And since he's not wearing his fucking birth certificate, I haven't a clue how old he is." She picked up his hand. "He has on a college ring. Harvard. Dark gold stone, I think, and some computer shit on it. Anything else I can't help you with?" She heard him sob and waited for him to compose himself. She knew before he spoke it was Keith.

"It's him. It's my brother. Is he... you said there was a breather. Is it him?" She told him it was. "Can you tell me, is he...what happened to him?"

She thought about telling him that he was in a fucking accident, but decided she couldn't walk that line. "He's the only one in the limo, probably because he's still wearing his belt. But the glass broke all to shit and he has a piece in his chest. A huge fucking piece, like I said."

She heard him sob again and felt her own heart take a leap. What would it be like to have someone care for her like that? But she banished that thought and looked up the hill to where they'd been driven off the road.

"There's a long stretch of highway out on two zero eight that's just after the big farm. You know where it's at?" He told her he did. "Good. They're about a mile down the embankment. You'll see...there's a body up near the road. One of the females that I guess was in this car. Don't hit her when you come through. She's suffered —"

She screamed out in pain. The man, Keith she supposed, had grabbed her arm when she went to touch his pulse again, and held her. She tried to jerk free.

"What's happened? We're on our way. Tell me what's going on." She put down the phone and tried to pry the man's hand from her, but he was holding her like she was attached to him. When she tried jerking again, blood poured from his wound and she stopped. She picked up the phone to hear the man cursing again.

"He's got my wrist, and I can't get him loose. Damn it all to hell." The man on the phone asked her to repeat what she'd said, his voice suddenly very calm. "He's holding onto me like he's never letting me go. I can't wait around here for you guys. I don't do police."

"I swear to you if you wait there I'll make sure you're not arrested. You've done me a huge favor by telling me what's going on. Please stay, and whatever part you had in the accident will not go to the—"

"Whatever part *I* had in the accident? Listen here, you motherfucker, I found them." She put her hand over Keith's throat and felt his pulse beating too slowly. "I'm going to save his fucking ass and then I'm out of here. You mother...fuck you."

She ended the call, then wiped the phone down. She was going to pay for this, she just knew it. Putting her hands on his chest, she knew that for as long as she lived she'd hate people. Pulling the glass out of his chest took effort, and she put her hand over him to start the process as soon as it was clear. When she dropped the glass down onto his lap, she heard the first sirens. She had to work fast now.

Closing her eyes, she gathered as much energy from around her as she could. Telling the deer that she'd captured in her snare that she was sorry, she took as much as she could from him without harming him, and he dropped to his knees. When she felt she had as much as she dared, she poured it all into the man's chest and felt the immediate connection to him as he took her in. His hand slid from her wrist, and she pressed more of herself into him. When she heard the first shout, she pulled back from him, drained. It was time to go.

He would make it now. Staggering to the open doorway, she fell out of the car and onto the snow. Reaching out again, she moved her power along the car and tried to think of everywhere she'd touched it. Moving away and deeper into the woods, she covered her tracks by floating just above the snow-covered ground, knowing that she was getting dangerously low on the ability to protect herself. When she made it to her shelter, she dropped to the sleeping bag and lay there. She had to stay awake in the event they found her.

Harley must have fallen asleep, because when she felt the tiger near her, she knew it was too late to run. She couldn't fight him if he wanted her, but she was going to certainly give it her best shot. When the door to her small makeshift home opened, she looked up at him. He didn't move and neither did she. The big tiger looked like he could eat her alive and wonder about dessert after.

"He's alive, right?" He nodded his massive head. "Then I don't suppose that I could persuade you to leave me the fuck alone and forget you ever found me. And if you know that fucking prick I spoke to on the phone, tell him to get the hell away from me before I really hurt him."

He looked to his left, and she knew there was someone with him. When a man stepped into view, she simply closed her eyes and shoved him away. It was all she had left. When someone pulled her from the shelter, she let them. When the same man picked her up, she cried out in pain.

"I'm so sorry. Come on, let me cover you up." She shook her head. "You're not going to stay out here."

"I am too." He laughed and she reached for more of the earth to help her. "You should put me down now."

"I'm taking you to the hospital. You're obviously hurt." He stopped moving and stiffened. "Is that you?"

"Yes." She touched his forehead with her finger, and he dropped her as he fell to the earth. She didn't realize that the cat was so close or she might have tried to fall away from him instead of on him. When he moved toward her, she put her hand on his fur and pulled energy from him. He dropped like the man had.

She figured she had about five minutes, less if there were more of them. Gathering just what she could carry, she moved in the opposite direction from where he'd been taking her. There was no time for her to try and levitate now, and she doubted she'd get too far the way she'd drained herself helping Keith.

She was moving into the river when the first pain took her.

You hurt my mate and now you're running away? Not good when all we wanted to do was talk to you. The woman's voice was as clear in her head as if she was standing right next to her. *He was only trying to help you.*

Blood poured from her nose as she stood up. Reaching deeper into the woods, she found a large family of deer and begged their forgiveness as she drained them. Then, focusing all her power back at the woman, she felt her pain. Smiling, Harley closed off her mind and willed herself away. They wouldn't find her now.

Harley fell forward again before she got more than a dozen steps. The pain this time was staggering. The woman again. When she tried to redirect her power back at her, Harley fell again, this time crying out. The woman was going to kill her.

Stay the fuck down before you hurt yourself. She sounded pissed off and for some stupid reason that made Harley smile. *I'm sending someone for you and you won't be able to harm them.*

Why the fuck don't you just leave me the hell alone? He'll live, and so will your fucking mate. I didn't do anything wrong no matter what that fucking moron said. She tried to stand again and the pain tore at her, but she got to her feet.

Christ, you're stubborn. And strong. I'm really sorry about this. The blow to her mind had her racing to the darkness. Using the last of her energy, Harley pushed back. As she fell to the earth, she felt the woman's pain and felt good about it. But there was nothing else, and she let the darkness take her.

~~~

Bronwyn fell to her knees and had to take several deep breaths before she felt like she could speak. She glanced at the shoes in her line of vision and knew it was Brock. The man would wear boots year round if he thought that Em would let him.

"You find her?" She nodded at him. "Ryland is going to be okay, and so is Neal. They have a hell of a headache, but they'll live. Want me to have someone go chase her down?"

"She's out, but I have no idea for how long. Christ, Brock, she's fucking strong." She let him help her up and he handed her a tissue. Her nose was bleeding and she'd not even realized it.

"I'm staying here until something clears up about the accident. I don't think this was slippery roads like the police are saying. They're taking Keith to the clinic. The team is waiting on him." She nodded. "Do you know what happened here, Bronwyn?"

She didn't and told him that. "I do know that whoever this girl is, she saved his life at a great cost to herself. I think...did you see that piece of glass? It was in him."

Brock nodded but didn't speak. They were all overwhelmed right now. She looked up when Ryland came toward her. He staggered a little but walked on his own. She wondered briefly if the girl had caused the accident, and knew that she hadn't. Something or someone had run them off the road and killed four of them.

Em and Jules went to where the girl was. Ryland pulled Bronwyn into his arms and held her while the medics worked on Keith.

"They said he was lucky." She nodded. "Do you know how lucky he was?"

"Yes. The glass that was covered in blood was in his chest, just like she said. He's lost a great deal of blood, but he'll make it. I don't know what she did but...those doors? She took them off to get to them, I think. They were tossed too far away just to have simply been part of the accident. She stayed with him, too." She looked back when she heard a door slam on the ambulance. "We'll follow them?"

"Yes. Mom is beside herself with worry, and Alistair is coming straight from the airport. He's picking her up. They're all going to meet us there. What do you think we should do about the girl? She knocked me on my ass, as well as Neal. What the hell is she?"

"I don't know. I was just telling Brock that she's very strong and very stubborn. I hope she is okay. I had to zap her pretty hard to get her to obey." She laughed. "But she gave as good as she got. Whatever she is, she's got a great deal of explaining to do."

Chapter 2

Harley woke quickly, something she'd done for longer than she could remember, and flinched away from the bright light. The man standing over her moved back, but not fast enough to avoid her fist connecting with his jaw. She sat up when he staggered back. Watching him recover, she reached out into the room and knew that there was at least one more person with them and he was a cat, the one that had picked her up.

"Where am I?" The man she'd hit, a doctor she assumed, glanced toward where the other man was. "I'm asking you, not him. I doubt he'd give me an honest answer anyway."

The doctor smiled and the cat answered her. "You're at the Fourth Street Clinic. And I've never lied to you yet." She snorted and looked down at her wrist, and found a deep dark bruise all the way around it. "Did my brother do that?"

Not answering him, she slid her feet to the side of the bed and dangled them over the edge while she tried to figure out if she'd fall on her face if she stood up. When she heard the door open and close, she didn't bother looking. She knew who it was, and she wasn't any happier with her than the woman apparently was with Harley.

"You're not strong enough to do whatever it is you're planning. And I don't think you should leave here until you're at least able to walk without falling on your ass." She felt her stir in her mind and pushed back. "You can't keep me out if I really want in."

Wanna bet, she thought. Standing up proved to be a huge undertaking. She wobbled a little and when she felt steadier, she let go only to grab the little dresser next to the bed. She made her way to the bathroom, holding onto whatever she could touch. When the doorknob was in her hand, she felt like she'd run a marathon.

"You had no identification on you when we brought you here. And I can't figure out what you are. I know you're not a vampire, but you're not human, are you?" Harley opened the door to the bathroom as the woman continued. "Can we at least know your name?"

"The man…the one in the accident? Is he going to make it?" She said that he was. "Good. Then there is no reason for you to hold me here longer. I'll be leaving, and if you think I'm going to pay for this room, you're fucking nuts."

"Can you please tell us what you know about the accident? My brother said it wasn't one. An accident, I mean. He seems to think that someone ran them off the road somehow." Harley didn't move or say a word as the man that had tried to carry her continued speaking. "We'd also like to know how you got there so quickly."

She turned to him then. She didn't want to get involved, but someone had run them off the road and left them all to die. The limo was going pretty fast for the road conditions, but the driver had it under control. She leaned her head against the door before she spoke.

"He's right. Someone in a dark SUV hit them several times in the rear until the driver lost control. The limo hit the guard rail three times before it jumped over it. The first victim was ejected before they were ten feet down. I didn't see what happened after that. I could hear it roll, but I didn't see it." She looked at him, avoiding the woman. "I didn't have anything to do with it. I was walking back from town to my home. Nothing more."

"I believe you." She laughed and went into the bathroom. She found her clothes in one of the little closets there and pulled up the gown she had on to look at her body, then dropped it again. She looked at her wrist.

He'd bruised her badly. She could make out each of his fingers along her skin, and there was a small tear on the back of her hand. She licked the blood off it and tasted the bitterness of it. She didn't bother looking in the mirror as she pulled off the gown and tugged on her damp clothes. She'd been in the snow a great deal, and thought that when she got somewhere to live again she'd have to find a laundromat.

She didn't expect to find the couple gone, but she was surprised to find others in the room. She could smell the tiger in one of the other men, and knew he was the one who had found her first. The woman had to be their mother. While they didn't take after her a great deal, she did smell like them. Harley sat down on the bed to put on her shoes.

"Are you leaving now?" She glanced at the older woman as she looked around the room. "I thought we'd made arrangements to have her stay with us. Someone didn't tell her?"

"*Her* is right here and *her* isn't going to stay with any of you." Harley stood up. "I'm sorry about the others in the limo. They were dead before I got to them. The other man—

you said he was going to be fine—I'm glad for that, but I don't owe you shit, and I'm out of here."

"But Keith wants to see you." She shook her head at one of the other men. "I'm sorry, miss, but he said that you're his angel and we only have him because of you. I'm afraid I'm going to have to insist that you at least go and talk to him."

She picked up her things that had been in the little closet along with her clothes, took out the little bit of money she had there, and put it in her pants. It was all she really needed anyway. The rest would have to stay because she had a feeling she was going to need both her hands before this was over. She looked at the big man, who now stood in front of the door.

"There are a great many people in this building that I can take what I need from. Are you sure you want to fuck with me? I'm not really what you'd call nice when I'm pissed off and cornered." He cocked an impressive brow at her. "You either move or I'll move you. And any of the rest of you who thinks you can stop me."

She started reaching for energy. There was a great deal of it here because of the incredible number of shifters. They had the most energy of anything she could take from. When she felt her body had more than enough, she lifted her hand and brought a small white ball of it out.

"You think you'll be able to use that on all of us?" She grinned at the man and nodded to the other men in the room. "Fuck."

She'd already taken care of them and the woman who was trying her best to bring her down again. Harley wasn't sure what she was, but she was pretty sure that she was something kickass. The only person she didn't touch was the older woman. She couldn't for some reason.

"I just want you to go and see Keith." The older woman smiled at her. "What's your name by the way? You had nothing on you when we found you that would tell us."

"I wasn't found, someone kidnapped me. And I'm not giving you my name unless you have a good reason to have it. Otherwise...." She shrugged. "I would very much appreciate it if you moved the fuck out of—"

She felt the power coming before he was all the way down the hall. Letting the ball go, she pulled it back into her body and took a step back. If this was who she thought it was, she had to go now. She moved the man she'd disabled quickly, not caring for how he'd landed on the floor, and yanked the door open, but it was too late. He was standing right there, smiling.

"I was just leaving. And I had no interaction with these people other than to save their brother. I'm ready to go." She dropped her head and was just on the verge of dropping to her knees when she heard him laugh. Lifting her chin, she glared at him.

"Hello, Harley. It's been a very long time." She moved back when he stepped to her. "Where did you think you were going so quickly?"

Years and years of training had her curb her tongue. Decades and decades of being subservient to this man had her needing to answer him. But she'd been banished. She'd been tossed aside from his palace and that of his brother and brought here as a punishment, because she'd been lied to.

"I'm leaving to where I wish to go." She heard the others come around and turned to keep an eye on them. "You've no say over me so long as I don't come to your attention. And I have not. I will leave here."

"Viktor, you know this woman?" The bitch again. "She's the woman I was telling you about that saved Keith. I wasn't aware that you already knew her."

"She was my...guard." Harley snorted. "Well, you were, my dear, for a great many years. And that of my mate. Will you now tell me what happened that day?"

When he cleared the doorway, she moved toward it only to encounter Peter. He simply stood there while she tried to think how to get around him without touching him. He smiled at her.

"May I get by please?" He waited for several seconds before he took a step forward. She took a deep breath because she thought she was going to get to leave, when he closed the door behind him and stood in front of it. Harley turned to Viktor.

"My lord, I would appreciate it if you were to allow me freedom." He sat down and pointed to the chair across from him. The men and women in the room stepped back. Probably a good idea if he thought she was going to have a conversation with him.

"Have you met the Goldens? They are by far the best group of weretigers I've ever encountered. This is Ryland and his mate Bronwyn. They are the male and female of this streak. Alistair and his wife Ally; Neal and his lovely wife Rayne are just there. Brock and his wife Em work for the Holders of the Realm. I know that you're acquainted with that organization. Jules and his wife...ah, there you are Lenny...they are the last of the children besides Keith, of course. And then there is their mother, Sandra Golden. She is a jewel, and you'll like her." Each of them either waved at her or nodded. "Everyone, I'd like for you to all to meet Harley Pennington. She is from my realm."

~~~

Ryland watched the woman as she continued to stand near the door. He had a feeling if it opened she would bolt faster than he could as a tiger. She was so stiff with her anger that he wondered what would happen if she let it go. He glanced at Bronwyn when she took his hand.

She's really pissed at him. Ryland told her he'd gotten that. *I don't mean mad like I was at her last night, but she'd kill him if she could and not care about the consequences. What do you suppose the history between them is?*

I don't know, but I'm thinking it has to do with something other than what happened last night. This anger seems old, like she's held it to her heart for a long time. Harley looked at Viktor and Ryland had a feeling that she was sizing him up. *What is she?* Bronwyn shrugged, and that did not make him feel good.

"I've done all that you've ordered me to. I've fulfilled my sentence ten times ten, as you've said. There is no reason for you to keep me here. I no longer answer to you or the Holders." She took a step toward the door and Peter straightened up. "I will be within my rights to harm you, Peter. Move or else."

"You'll sit down." Viktor's voice thundered in the small room, and Ryland felt the compulsion in it, but Harley only stood still. "I should like to have a conversation with you. I'm not here to do anything more than that."

Ryland felt Keith coming toward them. He was completely surprised by that, and more so when he came into the room and hit Peter. When Harley took a step toward the door, Keith snatched her back and pulled her into his body.

"Mine." He snarled at Peter, who took a step toward him and Harley. "What the fuck is going on here? I was…Christ, I'm not well."

As he started to fall forward, Harley caught him and helped him gently to the floor. A nurse was called for and several of them came running. Brock lifted him up and put him on the bed where Harley had been. When he turned back to see where she'd gone and get some answers, she was being held by Viktor. This was not good.

"I think you should let her go. I'm not sure what the fuck is going on here, but Keith is under the impression that she belongs to him, and we'll protect her from you if that becomes necessary. Let her go." Viktor held her tighter. "Viktor, I'm not kidding you. Let her go."

"She's his mate. And if you allow her to leave here, she'll never see him again. It has taken me nearly five hundred years to find her this time, and I won't have her running away again. She is very valuable to this family."

The room was tight with tension, and Ryland knew that one false move from anyone and there would be a room full of tigers and blood, maybe even a couple of bodies to boot. He looked at Harley and could see the anger boiling off her, and knew she was going to make or break whatever was going on here.

"Did you bond with my brother in any way?" She didn't answer, but he wasn't really surprised. She didn't answer anything. "I asked you a question. Did you bond with Keith in any way?"

"No." Viktor laughed at her. "I didn't. I...I can't have a mate. It's a part of my sentence. I'm to live on my own, fend for myself, and have no interaction with anyone, with the exception of a job to care for myself. By being held here you're violating my sentencing and I could be put back in...back to darkness, if not my death."

Ryland didn't know what the darkness was, but to see her shudder like she did made him think he didn't want to know. He looked at Bronwyn, then at Viktor. There was something very wrong about all this.

"Can you tell me what you did, then, to have Keith know you were in danger? He came here to protect you. There had to have been some connection made for him to know that." She flushed, and Viktor finally let her go. "What is it?"

"I saved him using…using my hands." She held them out, and he could see the long cuts in them. "I pulled the glass from his chest before I healed him. I might have…there was so much blood that I didn't think about mine mixing with his. He is feeling protective because of that only."

Ryland didn't think so, and he didn't think she did either. As he walked toward her, Harley flinched away from him. He held out his hands, and she put hers out again. She warned him not to touch her, and Ryland had no problem with that. There was another member of his streak that had the same issue at first.

"You should have healed them. Or can you do that?" She shook her head. "I see. You said you saved him by removing the glass. Then you healed him. That's why you were so weak when you tangled with my mate. I wonder what would have happened had you been up to full strength."

Harley put her hands behind her and looked at Bronwyn. "I would have killed you all. And she won't be able to do that now. I'm stronger and I've had rest. You had no right to invade my home or my mind. I did nothing wrong to you people."

"No, you didn't. But if you've started the bonding process with Keith, you'll need to finish it." She looked at him and he saw her panic. "Harley, no one will hurt you. I swear it. Neither I nor anyone in this family will allow it. But this thing with Keith, you know that I have to have you finish it."

"You've got to be fucking kidding me." She looked at them all. "Will you all stand around here and make sure that it's done properly? Or will you step out long enough for me to get his dick in me?"

"That's quite enough and very uncalled for." His mom moved to Harley. "You'll come home with me and we'll wait to see if this thing with you and Keith is anything more than...you'll not tell me *no*, young lady. I'm the elder here, and what I say goes."

Harley snorted again. "Elder? I think not. I'm a great deal older than you, my lady, and as I've said several times already, I can have no contact with you and your family. I would like to go."

Ryland nodded to Brock, and he moved to the door. There was something more going on here and he wasn't sure he wanted her to go just yet. When she turned to Brock, Ryland moved up behind her.

"Come here, please." They all looked at Keith when he sat up. "And if you guys wouldn't mind getting out, I'd like to have a word with her. Please."

Ryland moved to go around her, and the others moved as well. They were all out but him and the woman. He looked at Keith, then at Harley.

"You won't hurt him, I know that, but if he pisses you off like I'm sure he will, then just leave. I don't know if I can go through what I did last night again." She nodded but didn't move. "He's a nice guy."

"I can't be with him. You have to believe me when I tell you that it's dangerous for you all, especially for him, if you make me do this." Ryland nodded and left the room, closing the door behind him.

He wanted to hunt down Viktor and find out what the hell was going on, but from the sounds of things, Bronwyn had already started without him. The closer he got to the conference room, the louder the voices got. He stepped in to see his mom and Brock laughing, Alistair holding onto Ally, seemingly crying he was laughing so hard, and Viktor pinned to the wall along with Peter. Em and Rayne were sitting on the couch, and they both seemed to be in a great deal of pain, but not from anything more than laughing too hard. Viktor was about three feet off the floor, held there, no doubt, by Ryland's mate. Peter was sitting in one of the chairs, but he wasn't moving either.

"You'll tell me what you do or so help me I will tear you apart and feed your leftovers to the fish. Did you or did you not cause that accident?" Bronwyn tapped her foot, not a good sign. "I've had it up to my nose in half-assed answers from you, and I'll get them now or — "

"I did not have a thing to do with your brother-in-law getting hurt. Now put me down this instant." She banged his head against the ceiling. "You know very well that I'd never harm someone to get what I wanted."

"So you did have something to do with them coming together." Another bang to his head, and the man snarled. "You think you frighten me? Hardly. Tell me what she did to make her think she can't have contact with us. And so you know, you little pisser, you're not out of my line of fire either." Peter's head hit this time, and he opened his mouth, but Viktor cut him off.

"Put us down and I will tell you what I can." He hit the ceiling again before she set him down. "I should say that your temper is very violent. Whatever do you do when your mate makes you this mad?"

"He doesn't. You, however, did. That woman in there, what is she?" Viktor looked like he wasn't going to answer her, and she lifted him a foot off the floor. "I'm not fucking around right now. Tell us."

"She is accused of killing one of the royal courts." Viktor sat down. "It was a very long time ago, but.... I was able—recently, as a matter of fact—to find out that she did not. There was a...a lie told, and the person was not killed by her."

"A lie told? That's a must have been one hell of a lie. What the fuck are you doing here and not back where this happened and clearing her name?" Ryland waited for him to answer. "You can fix this, right?"

"No. I cannot. Not yet at any rate." Viktor rubbed his hand over his face and looked at him. "Should I take her back to our realm, she will be killed on sight. Should I go back without her, then she will be brought there and killed. There is no way for me to clear her name just yet. But her being with her mate will...help her."

"Help her how?" Viktor looked around the room, then at him. "Just who is it that she was supposed to have killed? I'm assuming from what you said that it was someone important. Who is it?"

"She was. Her name was Olivia and she was my mate."

Chapter 3

Keith looked at the woman as she stood so still. He'd asked her twice now to come closer, but she didn't move. He sat up on her bed and swung his feet to the floor. If she wouldn't come to him, he'd go to her. When he stood up, he had to hold onto the bed for several seconds to let the dizziness pass. He took the time to look at her.

She was lovely, even with the scratches on her face and neck. He wondered if she'd gotten them when she saved him, but didn't think she'd appreciate him asking just now. He moved slowly toward her, and when he was less than a foot from her, she took a step back.

"I won't hurt you." She didn't say anything. "I would…do you think I could touch you? I won't if you don't want me to, but I'd very much like to."

"Why?" Reasonable question, he supposed, but he didn't think she'd like the reason and smiled at her. "Your charm won't work on me, Mr. Golden. I'm not a pushover, and I'm certainly not stupid. Why do you want to touch me?"

"I want to see if your skin is a soft as it looks. I want to…I really want to taste your skin. Lick along your throat to your mouth and taste you there as well." She took another step back. "You won't let me?"

"Those are not reasons to touch me. They're more reasons for me to keep my distance. Do better or I'm leaving." He nodded and tried to think. She turned to the door.

"I could feel you. When the medics were trying their best to figure out how to get me out of the limo, I could feel your anger at Bronwyn. She was hurting you." She turned back to look at him. "And when she pissed you off here this evening, I could feel that too. I was coming to be with you when I felt your terror at Viktor—"

"I wasn't afraid of him." He watched her closely as she continued in a calmer voice. "I am not afraid of Viktor. He made me mad when he showed up here demanding that I obey him. I don't have to do that any longer."

Keith took a small step toward her. "You said you can't have contact with me. Why is that? Did he command it? I assure you that he won't keep us apart."

The second step he took made him stumble. He wasn't up to this yet and needed to shift to heal, but Ryland had cautioned him on that because of the others involved. The deaths of his friends would be questioned, and it wouldn't look good for him to be healthy just yet.

"There will be no keeping us apart because we're not going to be together. Period. I've no use for a mate or any male in my life. I like it just the way it is. I've grown accustomed to being alone. And I like it that way." He nodded and took another step. "What do you think you're doing?"

"Getting closer to you." The last step to her made him stumble again. He hadn't meant to fall so hard, but she caught him well enough. When she helped him to his feet, he didn't let her go. She looked up at him, and he could see that her eyes were the most amazing color of silver he'd ever seen.

"You shouldn't be up." Her voice sounded slightly husky and warm to him. "Let me help you back to bed."

His cock jerked hard in his pajamas. When he lowered his head to hers, she started to pull back, but he held her. Keith felt her breath on his lips and settled them over hers. Christ, he had finally had a taste of paradise.

She didn't touch him other than with her lips. She didn't pull away either, which he took as a good sign. When he pulled her closer to him, she put her hands on his forearms, but no more. Keith wanted to deepen the kiss, taste the dark richness of her mouth, but lifted his head instead. He wouldn't demand from her. Keith had a feeling she'd had enough people demanding of her.

Neither of them said anything as she helped him to the bed. When he was lying down, he closed his eyes for several seconds in exhaustion. When the light went off, he reached for her and grabbed her arm. As soon as she cried out, he pressed the button to turn the light back on.

"Who did this?" He moved his hand up her arm to see if there were other marks, but the ones on her wrist were the only ones. He looked up at her and saw his answer in her face. She pulled away and put her arm behind her.

"You were in a lot of pain. It's nothing." He asked to see it again. Reluctantly, she let him have it back. "It'll be gone in a few days, and it only hurts when it's touched. I didn't get out of the way in time for you not to be able to reach out to me. I...I tried to get away and I hurt me, not you."

"I'm so sorry. I never meant to...I had no idea that I'd hurt you." He pulled the injury to his mouth and kissed it. "I don't remember hurting you, but I can see that I did. I'd like to make it up to you."

She stepped back from the bed and stared at him. He wasn't sure what she was thinking, but he didn't think it was good. When she took another step back and started for the door, she stopped before he could beg her to stay.

"You're not like them." He was pretty sure she meant his entire family and not just Viktor and Peter, so he nodded. "They demand and tell me that I must do what they say. Why are you trying to be nice to me? Is it because you think that you'll get me to have sex with you? It won't work. I may not have a great deal of experience with humans, but I know that people don't treat me like you are. Not without a good reason."

"How do they treat you?" She looked at the door before looking back at him. "How is it that the others treat you, Harley? Was it my brothers? My family? Or was it Viktor and Peter?"

She touched the door handle but didn't open the door. "The king. He's Viktor's brother. He banished me here over two thousand years ago for a crime I didn't commit. Then he made me swear to the rules governing the crime as well. If I'm with you, even in friendship, then I will have to return to Ravengric to be killed. If you are my mate...."

"Then I would go as well and face the same consequences." She nodded at him. "Would you allow me to look into this for you? I could see what Viktor can tell me, and I'd very much like to hear from you what really happened at your trial."

"There was no trial. Mr. Golden. The king made the decision and I was put here. I had no say other than to leave. I never got to say goodbye to what was left of my family. You can do as you wish, but I'm not going to hang around to see what they do to me. I've been alone for too long to give it all for a man I don't need or want. It's much too dangerous for you anyway." He tried very hard not to be hurt by her statement, but he could understand it. "I'm going to be late for work. I wish you well."

She left him, and he lay back on the bed. He wanted to go after her, tell her that he could protect her and keep her safe, but he was barely getting around on his own. She didn't trust him, and there was a great deal hanging on the fact that if caught with him or any of the family, she would surely die. He looked at the door when it opened.

"You're in the wrong room." His mom sat down. "She's gone then? Will she be back to be with you?"

"I don't know. Did you know that she's over two thousand years old?" His mom nodded and he closed his eyes. "I think I need to talk to Viktor. She...she let me kiss her."

"That's a good start." She laughed a little and he looked at her. "One of your brothers would have had her bedded by now. But not you. I'm glad for that. I think she's...you should know that she's wanted for murder in her realm. She was accused of killing Viktor's mate. He says he knows now that she didn't do it."

He had no idea why but he believed that she wouldn't kill someone without cause. Keith felt his mom put a blanket over him, and his body relaxed. When the light went off, he opened his eyes again and spoke.

"Mom, she said if she mates with me and we all take her in as family, we'll have to go to Ravengric and be killed with her." He yawned. "That can't be right, can it?"

If she answered him, he didn't hear it. Sleep took him under, and he dreamt of a silver-eyed beauty that had long dark hair that saved him from a life of loneliness. Keith loved this dream.

~~~

Alfredo read the newspaper article three times, and every time he got a little more pissed off. The Golden brat had lived. Tossing the paper away from him, he saw it land on the obituaries and sneer at him as well. Golden's fucking name wasn't among the ones that were killed, and Alfredo was fucking pissed about that, so much he could see stars behind his lids every time he blinked.

"I just don't understand how he survived. The rest of them were killed almost from the start, and he managed to live? How is that fucking possible?" He looked at his enforcer, Carson Brooks, and growled low. He wasn't afraid of the man, but the growl did things to him that nothing else could.

"Hey, I did just what you told me to do. Knock the fucking limo off the road at that point. The only thing that they're going to find is a few scrapes of black paint on a black limo. They'll think the damage was caused by the accident, which was caused by the slick roads." Carson sat up straighter in his chair, and it was all Alfredo could do not to ask him to stand and turn. He had to think what they were talking about before he spoke.

"But you didn't do what I told you, did you? You were supposed to make sure they were all dead. They aren't. And the one that did live is the motherfucker I wanted dead in the first place." He stood up and paced. "Why the hell won't Golden simply sell out? I've offered him more money than the entire downtown project is worth. If he would give me what I want, then I wouldn't have to go to these extremes.

The son of a bitch has the buildings I want. What the fuck is up with that?"

Carson shrugged. "Could be he don't wanna. He built that place, didn't he? Maybe he has some sentimental value with it. Didn't his daddy used to work there, too? Not that I cared much for my daddy dearest, but there is something about having something of his. Even if it is just to piss on it once in a while."

Alfredo didn't really care what Golden's reasons were. He wanted it and that should have been enough. He didn't care for it when he was told *no* and usually made the person who said it to him pay dearly. But Ryland Golden seemed to be untouchable. He looked at the drawing he'd had made several months ago. It was his dream, the one that was going to leave his mark in this world.

Golden Towers sat right in the middle of the development he had found out about. And when all the buildings were ready to be purchased, there was going to be a great deal of money to be made on the ones that the city wanted to complete. Alfredo had bought all but five of the buildings. Three of them belonged to Golden; the other two to a man he'd only just found out about.

"Maybe he knows about this mall thing that's going in. Could be someone leaked it to him and he's going to hold out until the city comes to him." Alfredo looked at Carson as he continued. "I heard tell that the mayor is having all kinds of meetings with Golden. You think he's told him, sort of giving him that insider information like you got?"

Alfredo didn't want to think about that. If Golden knew, then he would never sell. And even though Golden was one of the richest firms, not to mention families, in the world right now, it didn't mean he wouldn't hold out for more money just to piss him off. He looked at the map and the five buildings that had sticky notes on them.

"Have we found this other man...Cook? What have you been able to find out about him?" Carson reached into his pocket, pulled out some folded sheets of paper, and handed them to him, and he looked them over.

"He's an old man by the name of Troy. He and some other guy, Marcus Cook, live nearby, but they use the building as a storage place. Seems he likes to collect. The older man, not the younger. I hear tell that they inspect their stuff more than once a week and are working with the Goldens on a few other deals. I can't really find out much about their finances, but I think they got some play money."

Alfredo looked up at him. "Collect what? Please don't tell me that he's only using the building as a storage unit for his stamp collection. That would really piss me off. That building is fucking huge. What can he be storing in it that makes you believe he has money?"

"Nah, not stamps. Troy Cook goes to auctions and buys things cheap. Then he...what did he call it? Oh yeah, he flips them. I talked with one of the antique dealers down in the District and he said the man can find just about anything he needs for his customers. And for the money? Not sure; they seemed to act like they have it but don't care. You know? Not like you. They sort of wear it like they're used to it. They been doing business like that for a few years now. The younger Cook, Troy, paints and reads. I figured them to be queer, but they're daddy and son."

Alfredo hated that word and the connotations that went with it. He himself was a gay man, but he knew that in his line of work keeping that to himself would make or break him. He moved to the couch and sat down. He wanted all those buildings.

"I want you to pay the Cooks a visit for me. You, not one of your flunkies. He's been avoiding me and I want answers." Carson nodded. "Be nice. I just want to know if he'll sell. And whatever his answer is, you bring it to me and I'll deal with him."

"So no fun for me." Alfredo nodded. "That sucks big hairy goat balls. But I'll do what you want."

Alfredo shivered at the comment. Where did he come up with these things? When he left, Alfredo got up to stand by the window that looked out over his yard. Christ, it was beautiful, and should be for what he had to pay to keep it this way. Like everything he owned, it was the best he could buy. Or steal. He wasn't above being ruthless to get what he felt he deserved. Going through the house, he smiled at all that he'd managed to collect in such a short time. When the butler cleared his throat, Alfredo turned from the Picasso and looked at him. He held out a small gold tray that held a small envelope. He took it without a word passed between them.

His partner was in the parlor. He nodded to the butler, and when he left, Alfredo went to the room just as Rocco was being given a drink. He genuinely liked this man and had since they'd met. But that did not mean that he trusted him. Alfredo trusted no one, save himself. Rocco Faulkner was a very wealthy and ruthless individual, and he'd taught Alfredo everything he knew.

"I read in the paper about the accident. Tragic. Too bad you didn't get your target." He sipped his bourbon. "Tell me again why killing off the younger man will get you what you want?"

Alfredo was served a drink as well and sat in front of the fireplace, and just then noticed the Christmas tree. He remembered the decorator coming in but not what the fuck she was doing. He despised Christmas and all the things that went with it. He made a mental note to have it removed.

"They're the closest family I've ever encountered. All of them live on the same estate and even though the other one — Jules, I believe his name is — had a beautiful mansion, he's opted to move back to the bosom of his family and live in a house that needs to be bulldozed and then burned to the ground." He sat up straighter on the seat. "I believe that if any of them are killed that Golden will be so devastated that Ryland will be easy pickings. It's how I worked the deal on this house."

"So you did. But to be honest with you, I don't think Ryland will be so easy to dupe. The man has a business mind about him that makes me envious. He's very well thought of as well." Alfredo shifted uncomfortably on the seat. "You should be more like him. It might get more doors opened for you. You need a pretty wife to hang on your arm at functions too."

"I'm not ready to settle down just now." And never would be either. This was another reason he drove to another state to have sex. This man would ruin him, and not only that, would more than likely kill him just because of his sexual orientation.

"You're getting too old not to be settled. People are already beginning to talk. You need a wife. I'll start looking for one." Alfredo said nothing. "What is your progress on the other buildings in the area? I understand that in addition to the ones that Golden has, there is another person of interest. Cook and...I can't remember. Do you know him?"

"Troy Cook. No. I've sent Carson to have a word with him." At his look, Alfredo spoke again quickly. "He's to only speak to him. I've made it clear that he's to not harm the man. I don't need another problem like before."

Carson had gone to see someone about another project Alfredo had wanted to get going. But the man had refused to see things his way, and Carson had taken exception to that. He'd nearly killed the man, beating him to submit, and had even hurt the man's wife. Alfredo had to pay a great deal out for that mess, and Carson had paid dearly as well. And the really shitty thing was that the project, like more and more they were doing lately, had fallen through.

"I don't know why you keep him around. The man is nothing more than a thug." He was, but Alfredo thought he was gorgeous and he liked looking at him. "There's no reason for you to have that type of man doing your dirty work. Not to mention he looks like he could easily fit the part of a gangster. Has he ever heard of blending in?"

The butler saved Alfredo from having to defend his man again. They both went to the dining room and were seated. This was his favorite part of having anyone over, the way that the servants lined the room as if they were in some Victorian novel. When the food was brought from the kitchen on silver trays, Alfredo thought of his own humble beginnings and smiled.

His parents would roll over in their grave if they could see him now. Had they had a grave, that is. The chains and cement blocks at the bottom of the lake held them in their final resting place, and he was a better man for it. Nothing to hold him back. He looked at Rocco when he realized he'd been speaking.

"I'm sorry. Drifting a little. What did you say?" Rocco looked upset at him, and his first instinct was to apologize again, but he didn't. This was his home.

"I asked you if you have had any word on when this project is going to go through. There are a great many of us buying up as much property as we can just on your word alone." He'd not told anyone to buy anything and had asked this man to keep it quiet, but that hadn't happened. "I think the group I have formed has just over ten million in this project that you said was going to make us all ten times what we invested. I don't see anything as yet, do you?"

"Not as yet. I told you that there is progress and it's moving along. And when I know something, you will. The city will need to make sure that the funding is in place before they can announce, which I would estimate within the next month...less if my sources are correct." He took a bite of his lobster and nearly moaned out loud. "There are two or so things that must happen, and I've been told those are in the bag. The old mayor going out, for one. He will be replaced as soon as Wednesday." That little project was a done deal too. He was having the man meet a horrific accident. There was no reason to let his wife not collect on the insurance, now was there?

Rocco nodded as he lifted his glass. Just as it touched the table with barely a sip missing from it, it was filled again. There were no slackers in this household or they were gone. And not just terminated either. The plates were cleared and small dishes of sherbet were sat in front of them. Alfredo didn't care for sweets, but he knew that this was part of the ritual that he wanted to maintain. He only ate one bite and waited for Rocco. He never realized that the man was a pig before. He'd eaten all his ice cream so quickly it was embarrassing, not to mention the small cookies that went with it.

And when Rocco opened his mouth to speak, Alfredo had to turn away. There was food hanging from his chin, and he was still eating the delicate shortbread. It took him several deep breaths before he could look back at him and answer.

"No. There are no more problems with the paintings. I've had an expert look at them, and they all passed inspection. He said that our newest artist is one that he'd like to keep for his own. Never had he'd seen a finer forgery." Alfredo leaned back when the final course was brought to them. He wanted this meal over with now because, to him, it had been ruined by his partner's bad manners. "We'll be able to fund a great many other projects once we sell those off. I have a buyer for two of them now and one lined up for another. I don't think it's going to make us, but it will help us get there."

After they were finished, they both went to the library. This was where they should smoke cigars, but since neither of them smoked, they simply drank brandy and watched the fire. There was a tree in this room as well, and he rang for the butler. This was enough.

"I'd like the Christmas decorations removed before I get back tomorrow. And if there are any cards in my mail, remove them as well." The butler nodded and left. Rocco didn't say a word, but it infuriated Alfredo when he realized he was being laughed at.

"Not in the holiday spirit, are you? I've a houseful this year. My children have decided to all converge in my home, and the missus is thrilled. We've nine grandchildren now and we've spent the national debt on them, I think." He chuckled a little, and Alfredo wanted to slap him blind. "You'll not be joining us again this year, I take it."

"I've made other plans." He hadn't, but it mattered little. There was no way he was going to be around children and their parents. Maybe he'd find himself a lover for the week and spend it with him. A good fucking was what he needed. He had to shift on his seat just thinking about it.

An hour later, Rocco left and Alfredo was at his desk. He picked up the phone and called Carson. The man answered on the third ring, and he sounded like Alfredo had awakened him. Alfredo's cock stiffened at the thought of waking the man another way.

"I want you to have someone pay a visit to the young Golden. He's still at the clinic, isn't he?" He told him he was. "Good. I want them to make it look like an accident. Men hurt as badly as him will need something extra in their IV, don't you think?"

"I'll get on it now. Oh, I'm going to see Cook in the morning. He and the younger one have just gotten back. They were on some fishing trip with some of their old buddies." Alfredo told him good. "I should have an answer for you by tomorrow afternoon."

"See that you do. And come here with the information. You know how I hate getting good news over the phone." He heard the man yawn and had to cup his cock before he hurt himself. "Come for dinner."

"Sure. But can we just have like a real meal and not all those different plates and forks and shit? Like a steak and potato and that's it?" He laughed a little. "You know what I mean."

"Yes, I do. And I'll see what I can do." He hung up when he yawned again. He leaned back in his chair and thought about Carson while he stroked his cock through his trousers. Christ, he needed to get fucked.

Chapter 4

Harley was bussing a table when she felt it. Stopping in the middle of the dining room, the hair on her neck danced and her wrist burned. She knew that Keith was in trouble as she set the tub on the counter. Then, moving to the manager of the dive where she worked, she told him she was going to be sick.

"Go then." She ran to the bathroom and pulled off the apron as she went. As soon as the door was closed, she moved to a stall, locked herself in, and closed her eyes. Shit. Someone was coming for him. She had to think fast, and knew that she needed to help him. The only person she knew that she could use, not to mention the only one she'd been touched by mentally, was not going to be happy. Closing her eyes, she willed herself to the kitchen of the bitch's home.

Both Mr. and Mrs. Golden were standing there. He had a little girl in his arms and both of them looked at her, startled. She didn't have time to explain.

"I'm sorry, my lord, but she will be safe." She put her hand over Bronwyn's and closed her eyes, and took them to Keith's hospital room. He was still sleeping. When Bronwyn started to speak, the door opened.

He's here to kill him. I need a witness. I need to make sure that no one thinks that I murdered without cause. Bronwyn nodded. *You'll stay here? Out of harm's way?*

Until I think it's necessary to step in. If he hurts either of you, all bets are off. I'll come at him just as you would, and we both know it. It was the best she was going to get, and she knew it. Bronwyn touched her arm before she moved away. *You'll have some explaining to do before we part company tonight, Harley. You understand that, right?*

Harley nodded and waited for the man to walk to the bed. He was dressed as a nurse…white pants and shirt, lab coat, and even a stethoscope. But it was the syringe in his pocket and the gun in his hand that had her moving up behind him. When Keith opened his eyes and looked right at her, the man turned. She pushed her power into his face.

The man screamed. She knew as soon as she touched him that she needed to stop, and she tried. But the hand on her shoulder made her drop the man to the floor and take a step back. Breathing hard, she looked at Keith and Bronwyn.

"Did he hurt you?" She shook her head at Keith. "Bronwyn? Are you injured? Did he hurt you?"

"No."

The room exploded with people. Harley took a step back, then another, and would have left, but someone grabbed her arm and she looked at Bronwyn. "Stay here. No one will hurt you. Not if they want to live. And try to keep your mouth shut, will you?"

They were both still standing there when Brock and Jules came running in behind all the nurses and doctors. Harley nodded to them both when they asked if she was all right, and waited for someone to arrest her. She'd not killed the man, but she knew he'd not make it until they figured out he was as close to death as it came without crossing over. He was just a human after all. The police were next.

"What happened here?" The officer looked at her, and before she could confess, Bronwyn stepped in front of her.

"We were visiting my brother-in-law when this man came in. He didn't say anything when we questioned him, and then he pulled the gun. Needless to say, we were both frightened out of our minds. But lucky for us he tripped. See…in that liquid there. I think it's from the syringe he had in his pocket." The officer knelt down and touched the man. "I think he was going to put that into my brother. Is that poison?"

To avoid looking at Bronwyn and hearing her fake, terrified voice, Harley looked at Keith, who hadn't stopped staring at her. They all knew that wasn't what had happened, but the police nodded. When they searched the dead man's pockets, they found a small vial of digoxin, a purified extract of foxglove. It might have been missed even if an autopsy had been performed.

By the time Ryland showed up, she'd given her statement three times and had been told that she was very lucky a dozen more. Brock and Jules never left her side, and Keith still hadn't said a word other than to tell the police he'd been sleeping and hadn't seen a thing. When the body was taken away and the police left, she started for the door.

"No, you don't. Come here." She shook her head at Keith. "Come here, Harley. I need to…I need you."

"I have to get back to work." She glanced at the clock over his bed and frowned. "It's probably already been discovered that I've left. I'm going to lose my job. I should go."

Ryland wrapped his arms around Bronwyn and nodded to the rest of the family. They moved out the door as if he'd ordered them to. He and Bronwyn moved to the door as well, but he turned and looked at Harley before he left.

"Did you know what he was going to do when you took my wife?" She nodded and started to apologize. "No need for that. You saved them. And had she not been with you...would you have told them what you'd done?"

"Yes sir. I killed that man. And I kidnapped your wife." She bowed before him. "I ask that you forgive me for involving her."

When the door shut, she looked up and realized that he'd not answered her. She turned to Keith, who was getting out of the bed. She took two steps back when he was near enough to touch her.

"I'm going to kiss you." She stopped backing up, her body not obeying her mind. "You brought my sister here. Is it possible for you to take us somewhere?"

"Yes. Where did you—?" His mouth covered hers, and she could only hang on. He wrapped his arms around her and lifted her to his body so that she felt every hard pulsing part of him. His tongue didn't swipe gently over her lips to beg for entrance, but boldly slid into her and circled her own. She moaned when he cupped her ass and rocked her over him, his cock so stiff that she wanted to touch him.

"Home. To my bed." He moved his mouth down her throat as he continued. "Now, Harley, take us to my bed."

She moved her hand up his neck to his mind to find it. When she realized where he lived, she wanted him to tell her it wasn't true, that the mansion he lived in wasn't his, but he nipped at her throat. And she took them there.

Her clothes were shredded by the time he backed her to the bed. His were in no better shape by the time she felt the mattress beneath her. He was touching her everywhere; his mouth, his hands moved along her skin so quickly she couldn't keep up. When he took her breast into his mouth, she arched up off the bed and cried out.

"I want to be inside of you. I want to come deep inside of you and make you mine." She nodded, her entire body feeling as if she was poised on the edge of a long cliff and he was her only rope line. As he lifted his head again, she looked up into his face and could see his need.

~~~

He watched her face as he plunged hard into her. She was tight, so tight as a matter of fact that he wondered if she was a virgin. Moving slowly inside of her, he kissed her gently on the mouth, then moved down her throat to her breast and suckled on the tip before taking as much as he could into his mouth.

"Please. I need you." He lifted his head and rolled his hips as she wrapped her legs around him. He wanted this to last, to bring her to peak over and over, but the more she moved under him, the harder he wanted to take her. Rolling to his back, he adjusted her legs so that she straddled him.

"Ride me. Take your pleasure and ride me." She seemed confused, and he pulled her hips forward over his and smiled when her face flushed. "You're in control. Take me before I lose myself in you."

Her hips moved erotically over his, and he held her until she seemed to get a rhythm going. When she put her hands on his chest, he reached up to his headboard and held on tightly so that he wouldn't rush her, wouldn't take her before she came.

Keith watched her breasts as they moved with her body. Her nipples, red from his mouth, begged to be suckled, and forgetting his promise to not rush her, he reached up and pinched them. Her back swayed, and he felt her tighten around him. Running his finger down her nipple to her belly, he skimmed over her pussy, not really touching; but still, she soaked him. Taking her offering to his mouth he moaned at her taste, and using his other hand, he pinched at her clit and she screamed.

Watching her come was like nothing he'd ever experienced before. Her face lit up. Her eyes, wide opened, seemed to glow in the darkness of his room. When he sat up and rolled her over, he wanted to come deep, but he also needed to taste her. Pulling from her body, he nearly took her again when she cried out, but he moved his finger inside of her and watched as she rode his hand.

"I'm going to eat you." She looked at him, wide eyed. "Taste your nectar. Then I'm going to come inside of you while your body is still coming. I want to mark you, love. Can I do that? Can I sink my teeth into you and taste what's mine?"

She was past knowing what he was saying to her. He could see that. When she cupped her breasts, he moaned and made his way down her body. As he licked her thighs, she lifted her legs and wrapped them around his shoulders. He spread her nether lips and suckled at her swollen clit.

"Keith," she screamed out his name, and he sucked harder, biting at her, tasting her as she cried out his name over and over. Sliding his tongue into her, he drank greedily. He let his cat come to the surface to taste as well, and she screamed out her climax as he growled. He wanted her, wanted not just to mark her but to drink deeply from her.

Later he promised him, later he could have her, but now he needed to take her. When she came again, her body as tense as a bow string, he moved up her, biting and tasting her as he went. When he was at her entrance again, he moved in slowly, this time feeling each ripple of her sheath as she accepted him. As soon as he was buried to the hilt, he licked a path from her pounding pulse to just behind her ear, and then took her lobe into his mouth.

"I want you to bite me when you come. Bite me and mark me like I'm going to do you." She nodded and begged him to finish her. "Soon, love, soon. Come with me, Harley. Come now."

He moved his hips, rolled them deep, and felt his balls tighten as they filled. He was so close that when she licked his shoulder he shivered at the feeling of the impending climax. When she sank her teeth into his shoulder and screamed around it, he cried out as well and bit her hard as his body felt as if it exploded inside of her.

Again and again he buried himself deep as she cried out over and over. Her nails raked his back as he bowed up and roared out a second climax, his body, his mind screaming for more. When she tightened around him again, he rode her through her climax, his own body spent. Dropping down over her, he felt her breath on his shoulder and knew that if the house were to catch fire right now, he'd never make it out. He was as good as dead. Closing his eyes to her even breathing, he rolled to his back and pulled her over him.

He was just drifting off when she spoke. He thought her to be asleep and woke up quickly when he felt her tears. Keith tried to think if he'd hurt her but couldn't remember her saying anything. He lifted her chin up to look at her.

"What is it, love? I'm sorry if I hurt you. I tried to be as gentle as I could, but you're...Christ, Harley you're so beautiful." She smiled at him and he kissed her again. "Please tell me what I've done."

"Nothing. Everything." He laughed with her, completely understanding her until she sobered quickly. "When he comes to gather me, he'll kill you as well. I tried to stay away, but you...you're much too male for me to have been able to stop this need."

"I won't let him hurt you, and neither will my family. We're mated now, Harley, a couple. I've marked you and have you in my bed. I think I could get used to this." She shook her head and cried more. "I was kidding, Harley. When who comes?"

No one was going to harm her now. She was his, and he'd kill anyone who thought otherwise. When she didn't answer him, he held her to him and ran his fingers up and down her back. This time he wasn't surprised when she spoke.

"The king. When he comes—and he will now—he'll be angry with me. Not that I give a shit about me, but...I don't want you and your family hurt. But it's too late for that now." She rolled over and looked at him. "He'll try, but I'm stronger than I was. I'll protect you all as best I can, but he's still my king no matter the distance."

Keith held her long after she fell asleep. He wasn't sure if he should be worried or not and wondered who to speak to. He decided his best bet would be his family, then maybe Viktor and Peter. He knew there was some history there but was not sure what it was. Taking a chance, he reached for Ryland. He sounded relieved to know where they were.

We were worried she'd taken you to the tent she's been living in. I don't think you can suffer that right now, not with your injuries. Is she all right? He told him she was his mate. *I know that, dork. When you take a mate, as male, I can feel it.*

Keith thought that was what happened but hadn't known for sure. *She said the king will come to gather her now, and because we've befriended her that we'll stand trial too. Do you know what that's about?*

Only what we got from Viktor, and that wasn't much. He said she'd been accused of killing his mate, but he knows now that it's not true. Ryland paused. *Bronwyn wants to know if you and Harley will come to our house for dinner tonight. She wants to talk to her. She thinks the girl is more than her, and she wants to find out what.*

So would he, and he said as much to his brother. *She's amazing. She brought us to my...to our house without hesitation. I think she figured out by searching my mind. Christ, I wasn't even ill like when Peter does it.*

I'm sure you had other things on your...mind. Keith felt himself flush. *But come to dinner tonight. We'll have the family over and see if you can get her to tell you what she is. Also, let her know that we'll have Viktor and Peter over as well. They might not like each other, but I get the feeling that Viktor has something to say to her.*

Closing the connection, Keith held her. He'd never felt this good in his entire life, and looked down at the woman in his arms. He didn't think she was asleep, and when she lifted her head to look at him, he rolled her to her back and settled over her.

"Hello there." She smiled. "I want to tell you a few things, but I don't want you to get upset with me. So if you find yourself wanting to hurt me, think of what we just did and how many more times we're going to get to do this in our lifetime together."

She tensed, and he curled his arms under her to hold her. He had a feeling she'd leave him, and he didn't want that either. He couldn't let her do that, not now. He kissed her mouth quickly and rested his head on his hand as he toyed with her nipple.

"Could you move in here with me? I know that you're living in a tent to avoid people, but that's not really...I could go live with you, but I'm thinking I don't have the strength to do that right now." He looked up at her when she snorted.

"You've strength enough to fuck me like a mad man. I think you could survive the cold. But you're correct, there's no reason for me to...I'm not saying I'll be easy to live with, but we'll try." She shifted under him and his cock jerked. "You've a way about you, don't you? I mean, you can have a great deal more sex than humans can. I've not had one, but I think they can have one good.... I've embarrassed myself."

He tried his best not to grin like a fool, but he couldn't help it. He'd never been called a mad man in the same sentence as sex before. But he looked at her seriously again. She simply snorted.

"There will be no humans or other beings in your life from now on. And I also spoke to my brother. He said he wants us to come over for dinner tonight. He wants to talk to us." Her nipple hardened under his fingers, and without thinking, he leaned down and bit it. She moaned at him. "I want you again."

"So I feel. We're going to break something important if you keep this up. Are all tigers like this? Wanting a woman after such a hard go at it?" He shook his head. "So it's just me?"

"Yes." He suckled hard again at her breast as she curled her fingers in his hair. "I have more to say, but I can't think right now."

"Don't then. You're making me ache again." Her feet moved along his calves and then wrapped over them. "Keith, I've…I was wondering if I could mark you as well. Claim you as you did me."

His cock lengthened at the thought of her making him hers, and he lifted his head to tell her so. But his breath caught when he looked at her. She had fangs, but not only that, he could see her ears weren't like his, not even close. There was a shape to them that made him want to suckle them into his mouth and moan. They looked like elf ears.

"What are you?" She shook her head and closed her mouth tightly. He moved up to enter her and slid home. "You'll have to tell me eventually. But right now, all I can think about is you marking me. Tell me what to do."

"I'm…Keith, if I mark you, you'll be mine forever. The king will—" He kissed her as he moved. "You need to let me drink from you here at your heart."

He nodded, his body already so close to coming that he was sure as soon as she bit him he was going to come again. Keith watched her mouth, waiting to see her teeth again. She smiled at him, and he saw them glisten.

"Christ, if you don't bite me soon, I'm going to die right now." She licked over his left nipple and suckled it into her mouth. Keith felt his balls come up around his throat. And when she sank her teeth into him, he screamed out, his climax tearing from him as if he were being torn inside out. When her wrist was put at his mouth, he sucked hard on her open wound and felt her blood fill his mouth over and over as he swallowed her down.

Keith was blinded by the intensity of his release. Stars rained behind his eyelids as he felt darkness close in. Every time he would swear he was finished, she'd move and he'd start again. When he finally dropped over her, he let his body start to slip away, knowing that for as long as he lived he'd never feel this way about anyone as he did her. He wanted to tell her, and with the last of his strength, he lifted his head and looked at her.

"I love you, Harley."

Chapter 5

Dakamon Ravengric woke screaming, his body drenched in sweat as his heart was pounding so fast and so hard he was sure he was dying. He nearly cried out again when the person lying next to him sat up. He sliced through her throat before he could think to stop when she asked him what was wrong. Not that it mattered to him if she lived or died, but he was terrified and didn't know what the hell was going on. Dakamon called his man to have her removed and his room repaired.

"See that the blood is removed from the ceiling this time. Last time it was there for a day, and it sickened me to think of the way others would perceive their king if they saw it." He moved out of the room to his bath and waited while his robe and clothing were removed. "Also, send me another. I want to feed from someone, and I might as well get a good fuck whilst I'm at it."

The man was just wrapping the body up in the ruined sheet when he turned to Dakamon. "Male or female, my lord? Or would you desire both again?"

He glanced at the male that was standing near the bed naked and turned away. He'd forgotten that he'd taken him to his bed and dismissed him. Dakamon told him "female" and to make sure she was well fed before she got to him. He didn't want to have sickly blood for his first meal.

He sat in the hot bath as his body was washed. The two women who did this were not to be bitten, but he could feel his fangs drop while he watched them bend over and pour the water over him. When the one nearest to him brushed her naked breast against his arm, he nearly pulled her over his cock and fucked her, but he'd never get another female to do this again if he did. Not after the last time. He reached for his man.

Bring me two, and make sure they are ready. I'm suddenly starved for both food and body. He stood up when they pronounced him finished, and they both stared at his cock straining from his body for several seconds. "Continue to look and I shall think you willing to suck me off. Otherwise, be done with it."

As soon as he was dried off, he heard the two women coming into his bedroom. They'd be ready for him, he had no doubt, and nearly whimpered when he saw them. Perfection. He nodded to the first one to take his cock in her mouth as soon as he lay back on the pristine bed. She was swallowing him down her tight throat before he had the other one's pussy over his mouth. Christ, he was going to come before he got to feed. When she cupped his balls, he commanded the one on his mouth to come, and he bit her at the same time. He loved the taste of blood and cum and drank deeply from her as the one at his cock brought him to climax. Sealing the wound at the pussy of the one at his mouth, he told her to ride him.

She slid over his cock with the help of the first woman. When she crawled over him and presented him with her lovely shaved pussy, he looked in the mirror over his bed and told her to eat the other one's pussy while she rode him. He bit her as well and fed on her as the two of them played. But Dakamon needed more.

Laying one down on the bed with her legs wide apart, he told the other to take her. She pounced on her pussy like he'd told her that it was a feast she could gorge on. Watching them writhe and moan over each other made his cock thicken again, and he moved up behind the girl's ass. As soon as he gathered enough cream on his fingers, he rammed them deep in her ass. Her screams made him harder. He wished now he had thought to bring another male to him. He would love to feel him at his ass while he fucked this one. Slamming his cock into her tight hole, he felt his eyes roll to the back of his head. Leaning over them both, he bit the one on her back hard on the throat and drank deeply while he fucked her partner hard.

When her heart began to slow, he didn't even bother to seal the wound, and lifted the other girl up from her pussy and bit her as well. Dakamon felt his climax race over him as she too grew dangerously close to death as he tore deeper into her throat. Not bothering with the bloodied wounds, he lay there until his cock no longer twitched, and then lifted from her as well. Going to the shower to wash them off him, he knew when he returned they'd both be gone and his bed once again made.

Washing his body hard, he thought of what had woken him. He'd never had such terror before in his rest and tried to think what had happened. As he reached for the towel that had been handed to him, he frowned. Something wasn't quite right with something, and it bothered him that he couldn't think what it was.

He was nearly dressed when a wave of despair overwhelmed him and he had to sit down. He didn't move as what had caused this occurred to him. She'd taken a mate? The guardian had taken a man to her bed?

"Not possible." He flushed when his man looked at him inquiringly. "Nothing. I was thinking out loud. The girls, are they both dead?"

"One is, my lord, and I do not expect the other to make it. I have also taken the liberty of making sure the male has been taken care of as well." Dakamon nodded. "Will you be going out tonight, sire?"

"No. Not right away. I have something.... Will you please have my brother called? I should like a word with him. Tell him that I will not take no for an answer this time."

Viktor had been avoiding him, a great deal more than usual. He had thought that by allowing him to go to the new world that he'd be out of his hair and he'd not have to look at him again. But of late he'd been hearing things, things that he didn't think were possible. And now he had to go to the new world and straighten some things out. Not to mention take care of something that had been left undone all those thousands of years ago.

Dakamon was looking forward to the visit too, not just to kill Harley but to see Viktor. He was going to make sure that his little brother knew that he was still in charge of him no matter where he resided. And that little prick Peter was going to be gone before he left Viktor, even if he had to kill him himself. He'd had enough of his meddling ways.

He was just being seated when the image of his brother appeared. The damned man looked like he'd been taking good care of himself, too. He was in better shape than Dakamon was, that was for sure.

"You've gotten fat, little brother. Didn't anyone ever tell you that a fat Ravengric was a lazy one?" Viktor said nothing, and that pissed him off. "Are you ready for my royal visit next week?"

"Is that coming up? I'd completely forgotten about it." Dakamon knew he was lying. "I suppose we can throw something together for you when you arrive. When is that again?"

He wanted to growl at him, but simply told him the dates. He might have thrown something across the room but for the fact that they could see each other. He decided that he'd played the concerned brother long enough.

"I will be sending someone to gather Pennington. When can you have her ready? She's broken her sentence and must now pay the price. Whoever she's taken for a mate will need to be brought to me as well." He watched his brother for any kind of sign that the two of them had been keeping company. "She's the woman who killed your Olivia."

"I know who she is. And also what she's been *accused* of doing to my Olivia. But how do you know she's taken a mate? I would think that between the realms, you'd not have that kind of connection." Dakamon had not thought of that. His brother would know as well as he did that there wouldn't be a way for him to find that information unless the two of them had been more than king to slave. They hadn't, but Olivia and the blood he'd taken from her was as good a connection as anything.

"Someone mentioned it." When Viktor started to speak, he cut him off. "You'll find her then, and the mate. I'll send you what I have on her from the last time that I had her looked up. When you have readied them, I will send a force for them. She will need to pay for her crimes now that she's broken the laws once again."

"What is it that you think she's done? Besides taking a mate, I mean. I only thought she was to keep from others of her kind. I do not believe that she's had any contact with anyone like her. I think it is safe to assume that she's the only one of her kind here." Dakamon felt his anger rise. How dare he, someone as low as he was in the right of birth, question him on the laws that he'd made?

"She's a murderer. If Father had not butted into the session and had her ordered to the new world, she would already be dead and no longer be a problem of mine." He stood up and so did his brother so far away. "Find her and ready her for her execution. I will not be made to wait any longer to have her dead."

"Dead? And how, brother dear, has she been a problem of yours?" Dakamon felt his fury pound at his veins as his fangs dropped. Viktor smiled as if he knew that he'd pissed him off, and he wanted to go across the realm walls and kill him too.

"I will not discuss this with you again. Have her ready." He closed the connection and could swear that he heard Viktor laugh. And worse yet, he thought that he'd heard Peter there as well. He hated that man.

Dakamon looked up when someone cleared his throat. His father stood there looking as if he'd heard every word that had been exchanged between his eldest and his youngest, and thought it funny for some reason. He came in without being invited and sat down. When he suddenly had a cigar in his hand and it was lit, Dakamon wanted to scream. It was going to be one of *those* kinds of visits.

"When do you plan to go to the new world and visit?" He knew as well as Viktor had. "I'm thinking I'd like to go."

"That won't be necessary, Father. I can take care of things there on my own." He nodded, and Dakamon started to continue when he was cut off.

"Be that as it may, I'm going too. And I wouldn't change things around to leave sooner to avoid me going. I have more allies in this castle than you do." Dakamon felt his body tense for whatever spewed from his father's mouth. "You'd do well not to kill another one of the servants either. They are here for our health, not for your pleasure."

"I thought living was my pleasure." His father's hand came out so quickly that he had no time to dodge from it. As it was, he had to pick himself up from the floor across the room.

"You may be the oldest, Dakamon Ravengric, but I am still lord here." He sat back down and waited for him to sit as well. He didn't even bother wiping the blood from his lip and nose. "I'm also taking your mother. It is high time she saw the world and met the family that sheltered us so long ago."

Dakamon wanted to scream at his father to please not bring up that ridiculous story again. He'd grown up with the tales of the Golden tigers and, frankly, thought about simply killing off the entire family just to say he'd done so. But his father was saying something else.

"I've taken the liberty of finding you a mate. You'll not have children by her, but you need someone you can keep around to feed from permanently. No more killing of the staff and no more sex with anyone who has any opening you can stick your dick into." The cigar disappeared, to be replaced by a glass of blood. "You'll be full king if things go the way you plan, and I'd like to—"

"What do you mean full king *if* things go the way I plan them? I am the king of Ravengric." Or would be if his father would let go of the reins and leave him the fuck alone. "You retired and I took your place."

"You've taken no one's place, and to retire would mean that I do not have to return every other day to bail you out of one issue you've caused after another. You've been a failure as a king thus far." His father stood up and glared down at him. "You've got a great deal to answer for, I think. One of which is this girl. What sort of hold does she have over you that makes you think to kill her? A hold that's strong enough to have you think to go to the new world to have it taken care of."

"She was forbidden to find a mate." His father shook his head. "She was told that finding a mate would be her certain death. And what has she done but broken every other rule we put before her, and is now not only mated but, mayhap, claimed him as well. I cannot have her breeding more of her kind into this world."

His father didn't say anything for several seconds. Almost a full minute went by before he finally did speak. "You cannot keep her from her fate and finding a mate. And she was told not to be with her own kind. As Viktor has pointed out to you, she isn't with her own kind. What have you done to her, Dakamon? What lies have you told her and, apparently, Viktor, that you did not tell me? Or, for that matter, what have you told her that you think is more than what I have decreed?"

The pain in his head started almost as soon as his father spoke. He felt him rape his mind over and over, unlocking places that Dakamon had long buried. When his father sat down again, he could see that he'd found it all...found every little thing he'd done since he'd been born. His father stood and glared at him.

"You are a monster. Not only that, but I'm ashamed to call you my son." Dakamon raised his chin, daring his father to say whatever was on this tip of his tongue. "You are hereby stripped of your duties to replace me. As of this morn, you'll be taken to the family house and I will step back into place as king. You'll not be allowed to go on. You'll ruin us if this ever gets out."

As Dakamon stood up, he felt the magic and power he'd been given by his father start to fade. As they weakened him, he knew that his father meant every word he said. Before the shackles could be bound around him, he said the words that would take him where he needed to go...to the new world. A place as far from his father's sentence as he could get and still be able to take care of the one person who had been his downfall. Harley Pennington had to die.

His home he'd bought only weeks before for his visit was nice, but not his castle. There were servants in place, but they were not used to him and his ways. The first thing he did was grab the little maid coming down the hall toward him and take her throat. Christ, he was a fugitive. And one without much in the way of power in a world he knew nothing about.

~~~

Harley watched his family. They actually terrified her to no end. She knew that she could kill them if it came to that, but they were simply too...everything. Noisy, nosy, and even too close to each other. Every time one of them walked by another, they'd be pulled into an embrace and hugged tightly. She'd been hugged in the same way several times already. She took a step back when Ryland looked as if he was going to do it again.

"You'll behave, my lord, or I shall resort to hurting you. Go and touch one of your own kind." He laughed at her. "I mean it. You're all too touchy-feely for me. I like it when I am left alone."

"You've held my daughter and didn't seem to mind that too much." She glanced at the little girl, who seemed to enjoy being tossed in the air by Keith. "And I'm sure you don't turn Keith away when he wants to touch you."

"If you're referring to sex, then no, I don't. I've never had it before and I think I quite enjoy it. And I should like to enjoy it as much as possible before the king of Ravengric comes to collect me." She looked at Keith as she continued. "I will beg for his life if possible. I don't want anything to happen to him. If that fails, I will try to hide him away."

The door to the room where they'd been gathered opened, and she brought up her shield as soon as Viktor and Peter came into the room. Both men looked right at her, and she had to fight hard not to bow. She'd been away from Ravengric for a very long time, but it mattered little. Showing them respect came as second nature to her even if she didn't believe that they deserved it. Viktor stood before her, and she didn't move.

"I have something to say to you. I would like...could we talk, please, without you wishing me dead?" She shook her head and Ryland laughed. "I suppose I deserve that. But what I have to say is very important to you. As well as to Keith. I hope it will keep you from being killed when Dakamon comes here."

"He comes? Soon?" Viktor nodded and she felt her legs weaken. "When? I should like to know when so that I can try to devise a plan to save this family."

"I've been working on that for...may we please sit and talk? What I have to say concerns all the family, as well as you." She didn't want to, but it wasn't her home. Ryland nodded and everyone took a seat when he asked them too. Peter stood beside her, and she took a step back from him when he put out his hand.

"You will not be harmed by him, not again. This to you, I swear." She only stared at Peter. "I have…I should have believed you."

"Yes, you should have. And you should have believed her." He nodded. "I want you to know that I plan never to forgive you. And that when the king comes, I will know that my death is on your head. You could have saved Olivia, but you chose to side with the king, a man who should have been drowned at birth."

She looked to her right when she heard a sharp intake of breath. She looked at the women standing there and knew that they were Peter's friends. But Rayne looked like she would hurt her. When the woman took a step toward her, Peter stepped between them.

"I deserve what she says. More so than any of you could ever believe. I…I should have done more than…." He looked back at her, then at the women. "You will hear soon enough what I've done to deserve what she feels for me."

Harley looked at Viktor and he nodded. "No," she told him. "You've no right to air out what I have been…there is no reason for them to know how I brought shame onto your household."

"There is, because you were not guilty. You did tell us you did not kill her, but…." Viktor looked around the room. "I will try and tell you what I've only just come to find out."

Harley tried to reason why he'd say such a thing to her, and couldn't think beyond Peter having defended her. She looked at Keith when he touched her arm. He smiled at her, and she had an overwhelming need to run. As if he knew her feelings, he curled his arm around her waist and held her. She looked at Peter when he cleared his throat.

"In a few short days, the king will be here in this realm. I've heard from someone very close to the household that he plans to come here to check on the progress of his brother. Viktor had things—jobs—he was to do when we came here, and his brother, the king, has decided that he'll come here now and check on him." Peter looked at her. "He has also ordered Viktor to gather Harley and her mate so that before he comes here he may carry out her sentence and have her and her mate beheaded. He thinks to have you both killed in Ravengric."

She did sit then. Keith was saying something to her, but she couldn't hear over the pounding of her own heart. Death by beheading was the only *true* death for her kind, and she knew that meant that as soon as the king saw her, she'd get no chance to plea for Keith's or any of the other Goldens' lives.

Harley looked at Viktor. He was her only hope in saving her mate. She stood up and walked to him and lay at his feet. Tears burned her eyes even as she begged him to help her. She looked up at him when he bid her to speak.

"I will freely admit to the murder if you save the Goldens. All of them. I will say that...I will write out my statement now if you wish. Would you...give me the words and I will put them to paper for you and...Lord Peter?" She looked into Viktor's eyes when he lifted her chin. "I will do whatever necessary to save them."

"Of course you will. That is why we saved you until last, my dear. The only way that we can defeat Dakamon is with all of you women together." He smiled and she frowned. "You have been through so much, Harley Pennington, more than any one person should have been. But you'll see it will be all right now. And my brother will not harm you."

Chapter 6

"Before I left for this world, I had Peter come here over the course of several decades. During those times, he would keep close tabs on one of my very dearest friends. He was coming here long before any of us knew of the connection between our world and this one. Peter was…Peter was the only man I've ever trusted until now." Viktor looked around the room, thinking that these people had come to mean a great deal to him. "My mate, Olivia, had been excited to start a life here. We were going to meet up with our friend and his new family and live out the centuries watching the world as it moved by us. But Peter was…. Perhaps Peter should tell this part."

Peter stood up and glanced at him before he picked up the story. "Long ago, I met a man who took a tiger to his own. She was a real tiger and not a shifter, as he was. His father, the king of another realm, said that they were not to be together, that as his only son he was unable to carry out the duties of the—"

"Oh my God." They all looked at Sandra when she stood up. Viktor had known she'd get the reference before anyone else. "You mean the male? The one that brought me the babe all those…he saved my Brock and…. All this time you've known of us and the legend that is as much a part of our family as...well, as you are?"

She sat down and stared at the two of them. Peter waited until she nodded, but before he could continue, Brock stood up and looked his best friend in the face. Peter didn't flinch, but Viktor could tell that he waited for a blow from the larger man.

"He gave me this beast? The one that has for many years nearly torn me apart?" Peter nodded and told him it had been his idea to do so. "Fuck you."

Peter didn't fight back when Brock hit him. He could have and would have been justified in subduing the younger man, but he let him hit him again and again until Ryland pulled him off. Brock jerked from his brother but didn't go near Peter again. Brock sat next to Em and held her to him. Viktor had no doubt that once they heard the entire story that he'd forgive Peter for everything.

"It was necessary or you would never have survived. You were...when he bit your leg, it was to pull you to safety, but you were already dying. I could have saved you by stepping in, but it would have taken too much interference and you very well might have died anyway. The tiger bit you and saved your life." Peter sat down as he continued. "You'll see when we have told our tale. I swear to you it was necessary in order to save you all."

"So you've been meddling into our lives for decades." Ryland didn't ask, but they both nodded anyway. "All this time...all this time you've been playing us like men on a chessboard, moving us to suit yourself."

"No. Not quite. I started this to save you because of the care you and your family gave to a small tiger. But when he took your blood...." Peter looked at Viktor and he nodded for him to continue. "When he took your blood, he knew that you were a part of more than just this realm, but the one he'd come from as well. Our world."

"Legend says that the cat once roamed the castle without fear of harm. He was greatly revered and loved. I myself had brushed his fur when he sunned himself. And though it was not my duty, I did feed him the choicest meats because he'd been...he was magical." Harley looked at Viktor as she continued. "When I was accused all those decades ago, he would not let your brother kill me, but stood in front of me until your father came to see what the commotion was about. I didn't even know until I was sentenced. The tiger nearly attacked Dakamon when it was decreed that I come here."

"You told us that she was accused of killing your mate. If you were coming here, then what the hell happened?" Bronwyn smiled a smile that he'd seen her use when she'd had enough nonsense. "The short version if you don't mind. I would like to fix this before it's too late."

"You told them?" Viktor nodded at Harley when she stood up again. "You swore to me that no one would ever know unless I told them. You lied to me. You motherfucker, I should kill you."

She took a step toward him, and he raised his hand. She stopped instantly. When Keith stood up as well, he stopped him too. The two of them were going to be difficult to hold. He was having trouble holding them now. He couldn't wait to see what they did when they were really pissed off.

"We'll never get this tale told if I have to spend my time placating the two of you. You're...." He stood up and went to them. "My God, you've done it. You've claimed him."

Harley broke free of him and stood in front of Keith. She was much stronger now than she'd been before, and he knew that it was because she was feeding from the others in the room. She raised her chin, and Viktor took a step back from her anger.

"He is mine."

Viktor nodded, afraid of her more than he'd thought possible. Then he smiled, even though he was more than a little afraid she'd take it the wrong way.

"You'll not harm him or so help me, I will kill you. I didn't kill your mate, but I will kill you if you harm mine."

"No, you didn't kill my Olivia. Dakamon did." She frowned at him. "That's right, and I'm pretty sure you were aware of that. I didn't know it at the time of your sentencing, but…. Perhaps we should begin again."

"I was wrong in accusing you." They all looked at Peter. "I took the word of someone I no longer trust and accused you wrongly. The king…Dakamon told me that he'd seen you covered in blood and that you'd threatened him. I believed him because he is…*was*…my king. I would beg your forgiveness."

Viktor didn't think she would give it. In fact, when he felt her raw power surge up a little, he thought for sure that she was going to kill him. But Keith put his hands on her arms, and she visibly relaxed as well as pulled her power back. She nodded once to Peter before she walked away. When Keith started to follow her, it was Bronwyn who stopped him.

"She needs a minute. Give it to her and you'll be better off."

Viktor looked out the doorway Harley had gone through and heard a loud crash.

"She's blowing off steam, and there is nothing in that room that can't be replaced or fixed."

Keith nodded but didn't sit. He watched the door until she came back. They both sat on the couch together holding hands.

"My mate Olivia was a beautiful creature. And I counted myself lucky that she'd been my mate every day." Viktor thought about his lovely mate before he continued. "She was ill tempered when it came to me at times because of my brother. She thought...she knew, as it turns out...that he was evil and not at all suited to being king. She'd even gone to our father about him. And that was what eventually destroyed her."

"So that's why he killed her?" Viktor had been looking at Harley, and Ryland's question startled him. "Your brother? You said he killed her, is that why?"

"No; he did kill her, but not because she'd gone to my father. We believe he killed her because he wanted something from her and she wasn't going to give it to him. He wanted her in his bed." Viktor continued to watch Harley to see if what he and Peter had figured out was true. "He even tried to have someone else bring her to him, and that person refused. Didn't you, Harley?"

"I...she begged me not to tell anyone. Made me swear it even though I wanted her to go to all of you, but she was embarrassed of what he'd.... He said things to her that were not true. I could not go against her in this. She made me...she said it would only cause more problems, and she had a plan to make sure that no one knew and that he'd be taken care of." She looked at Peter then, and then back at Viktor. "I did tell Peter that morning. He had come to me when I'd been in the infirmary looking for her and had asked me what had happened."

"You told me that the king had tried to kill you. You said that he'd ordered you to bring Olivia to him and to tie her to his bed. You refused and he tried to kill you. You were badly injured at that time." Viktor nodded at Peter to continue when he looked at him. "You told me, and I said for you not to lie to me again, that saying such things would get you beheaded. But you didn't listen."

She'd gone to Viktor as well, but he too hadn't heeded her story, and had blown her off just as Peter had done. "None of us wanted to believe that the king would do such a thing...not my own brother. We'd all been duped in this. Even Father."

"What happened to her?" He looked at Rayne. "Your mate was raped by him anyway, wasn't she? And then killed?"

"Yes, but it was much more than that. She'd been brutally raped over the five days she was missing, you see. He'd...I didn't know where he had her hidden, but I do know that Harley searched for her the entire time, never sleeping. Our connection was blocked because of where he held her, below the grounds. My own guard was looking as well, but they looked beyond the kingdom while she searched within the walls. When she was found...." Viktor felt his grief as if it was as fresh as the morning sun. "When Harley found her, she was already dead. I believe that she tried to bring her back to me, but she only succeeded in covering herself in my Olivia's blood. That was how Peter found her, leaning over her body using her magic."

"So he accused her unjustly and everyone believed him." Viktor nodded at Keith. "Was there no trial? No one to stand up for her?"

"No. She was sentenced to this world before I could…I was in grief and could not come to her aid. She was sent here before I could even collect my Olivia's body."

"Dakamon wanted me gone." Everyone turned to Harley, and Viktor held his breath as she looked at him. "You knew that he wanted her, didn't you? She knew it. My lady knew it before you and she were mated. That's why I was brought to your home to protect her. But in the end, I failed you both."

"Nay, child, we failed you. Several times it was you who showed us all what sort of monster he was. And still we believed us safe. You're the one that was harmed the most in all of this. You were sent here without friends, without any contact with your…. I'm so sorry about your family. Every day I wish I could have done something for them. But like you, they were all sentenced before I knew what was going on." He stood up and walked to her to bow before her. "Your mother and father…I cannot tell you how sorry I am for what was done to them."

"He killed them too?" Viktor didn't bother turning to Ryland when he asked, but nodded. "Mother fuck, that is some screwed up system you have over in your realm. I'm glad that I live here where things are run just a little better."

Viktor now had to tell her what had happened not an hour ago. He glanced at Peter, who nodded once, then at Keith. They were going to need his help too. He finally looked at Harley

"He's here." Harley stood up, nearly knocking him over. "He arrived not long ago. We don't know where precisely, but were hoping that we could find some records of him purchasing land close by. It would have been within the last ten days, but not much more."

Keith left the room, only to return a few minutes later with a laptop and a large satchel. He was already clicking away on the keyboard before Viktor could say anything more.

"There have been several homes purchased within this area over the past six months. Most of them have had a loan taken out for them. Two...no, three of them have been paid for with cash." And just like that, Keith narrowed the field down to three names rather than the four hundred that Viktor and Peter had found.

Keith asked several questions while Harley paced. When she turned to Bronwyn, she smiled. Viktor didn't care much for that smile; it reminded him of a shark, a hungry shark.

~~~

"I need you." Bronwyn snorted at her but stood up. "Do you think I can have a little of your juice? I can work just a little faster than that thing."

"You drain me and I'll kick your ass anyway." Harley nodded, knowing that if she drained the woman to nearly nothing, she'd still manage to hurt her. "Tell me what you need and I'll try to help."

"I just need a little of you. Like...like an electrical plug. I can reach really far, but I need more than...I don't want to hurt Keith." They both looked at him, and he looked back. "I'm going to find him, and he'll figure out where we are. But this will work. I need for you to track where I am."

"How?" She looked at Keith when he asked. "How will I...? I guess I don't understand. You want me to track you? You're not leaving here. Not without me."

"I'm not; you just need to keep up with me via our connection. I need you to come along, but we're not leaving. I'll show you landmarks or whatever you want to figure out where he is. I won't know what to look for, so you're going to

76

keep up with me so we can find him. I can...see him, but not know enough about how to find him." She looked at Viktor. "And he's going to be our beacon. You'll let me touch you, won't you, my lord?"

"Okay, one thing first. What the hell are you?" Bronwyn looked at her, then smiled. "I know you're not what Peter and Viktor are, but you aren't just your run of the mill powerful person either. What the fuck makes you so...special?"

Sandra laughed, then stood up and came to her. "Haven't you all figured it out yet? I'm surprised at you all. She's her sister, Olivia's sister. And you're some sort of guardian, aren't you? More powerful than even the king and Peter."

"Yes, my lady, we both were, my sister and I. We had all the power we needed to keep the others safe. Our family has been the guardians of the realm since the realm was created. My sister was...she wasn't nearly as strong as me, but she wasn't without her own power. It just wasn't enough to fight against what she had to endure. I should have been there to save her." When she started to turn away, Sandra pulled her face to look at her.

"What would you have done differently? What could you have done that would have been any more? Killed him? I don't think that would have helped her or you. Would you have gone to someone else? That didn't help you either, did it? You did what you could, more than anyone else could have done. You found her for Viktor, and then you came here to us."

Harley nodded and looked at Bronwyn. She had to take several deep breaths before she could speak. Bronwyn seemed to understand and waited. When Harley was composed, she looked at Keith.

"I'm going to search for him using Lord Viktor. When I find him, you'll touch me and see where we are. I'm not sure what you need, but hopefully you can get something." He nodded, then stood up and kissed her on the mouth. She needed that more than she'd realized. Harley looked at Viktor and put out her hand. He had to touch her or the connection wouldn't be complete.

As soon as he put his hand in hers, she felt Bronwyn wrap her hands around her arms. The power was amazing, and she cried out with it. When Rayne stepped up and touched her as well, Harley felt as if she'd stuck her finger in a light socket.

There were memories there, some them as vivid as if she'd been with them when they were made. Others were faded but still no less meaningful. The women had become fast and powerful allies.

Neither of the women would let her go. She knew this when she reached out to find the man who had both ruined and completed her life. She would never forgive the king for what he'd done, but she would always be grateful for him giving her Keith.

Her mind began to connect to the king through not only the connection as her former king, but also because he'd bonded with her sister through the rape. It was all she could do not to go to him and kill him now. There were images of Olivia in Viktor's mind, and she tried her best not to dwell on them overly much. When she found the connection, she stopped and listened to the conversation that he and Viktor had had recently. She used that one to connect to him.

Image after image moved by her. She followed him from that point on and found the argument he'd had with his father and him leaving the realm. She started to pull from

Viktor, no longer needing his connection now that she had her own, but he tightened his hand around hers. He would need to know, she supposed.

When she found him in a house, she reached out for Keith. He gave her a surge of power she'd not expected, and she could see the house. There was any number of clues, she supposed, in what she was sharing with him, but nothing she could use. Dakamon was pacing the grand hallway and muttering to himself. Using some of the extra energy, she moved beyond him to the outside of the building, then onto the streets and over the city that seemed to flourish despite what was living near it.

Streets and other houses were there, cars with license plates on them. Going closer to a few of them, she paused. When Keith seemed to nod at her, she moved to the building across from the one the king had been in. When she felt a little weaker, she started to pull away. Then another surge of power came to her. Moving further down the avenues and buildings, she found more addresses, as well as people.

Go to the yellow box there on the corner, the one next to the mail box. It will have information on it as well. She was so startled by Keith speaking to her, she nearly lost the connection. *We have you, love. Go to the box and let me see what's in it.*

She moved closer to it and looked. The Columbus Dispatch with today's date on it was on the top. She looked at the other boxes there and found other papers with today's date, as well as a few more Ohio papers. He was that close to her and she'd not been aware. Harley started to leave but decided to go back to the king.

Dakamon was with another man, and neither of them looked all that happy. She shadowed in the room and stilled.

"You should know that I've been keeping tabs on him for decades. He's not a man who lives well, is he?" The other man laughed as he continued. "As for the girl, I can't find her because she's no longer where I left her. I think she might have moved on again. But she'd been here in Ohio, same place as your brother."

"So he's had contact with her?" The man shook his head. "Then how did they end up in the same state? Magic? I think not. He gave up his power when he decided to run here with his tail between his legs. You keep looking for that bitch. And she'll have a male with her now. I'm not sure who or what he is, but she's taken a mate and I want him dead too. I can't have her breathing when my father comes here. He'll find out too much and I'll have to figure out a way to kill him as well. I want my kingdom back, and he needs to be out of the way."

"Will you be going after your brother then? I can have him brought to you when I find him. It's just a matter of time. I'm sure that when your father finds out that you're here too, he'll come after you. And thanks to you, isn't Viktor next in line for the throne?"

She felt Viktor's pain and felt badly for it, but before she could pull from the two men and their conversation, the king...former king, she supposed now...spoke again. The fury in Dakamon's voice was obvious.

"I'm not going to give up my kingdom, you stupid moron. My father will not give me what I want, and he too shall meet with an untimely death. They will all understand soon enough that I'm going to lead, and they'd better fucking well follow me or die like the rest of them." The other man snorted. "You find my plans to be funny?"

"No. What I find as funny is you think you can win this. Especially against your family. And that woman. She's not going to let you get by with shit again." He laughed again. "And if she finds out you're here, then…her powers weren't taken, remember?"

"I'm not concerned with her, I never have been. As soon as I find her, she'll be bowing before me as I slice off her head. It's too ingrained into her DNA that she needs to do as I say. No, I'm not afraid of her. She is by far the least of my problems."

"Yeah, well, that worked so well for you before."

Harley knew that Dakamon was going to kill the being and couldn't do anything about it, not in this current state. Actually, she wasn't all that sure she would have if she had been there in the room with them. She watched as Dakamon lifted his hand and pulled from his mind before he could deliver the blow. She sat down hard when she stepped away from Keith and Bronwyn. That's when she noticed Rayne along with Em. They'd helped her too, apparently. She looked at Ryland.

"I would like to finish speaking before you fly off the handle please." He raised a brow at her and smiled. "Let's just assume for a moment that I'm a little stronger than you are and you realize that I'll make you listen if you don't agree. It'll probably go a good deal better for you if you just do it."

"I do not fly off the handle." Five people burst out laughing, and Bronwyn snorted again. "I don't. I get frustrated when things don't go my way, and I take it out on everyone. That's not flying off the handle. That's…it's just the way I am."

"Whatever. My suggestion is that you let me handle the king on my own. I can do it regardless of what he says." She stood up when she felt the room tighten. Before she could ascertain who was coming, she'd already dropped to the floor and lay very still. When the man chuckled, she didn't even bother looking up.

"You are a very brave and wonderfully loyal woman." She peeked up at the man towering over her. "You should really get up and introduce me to the room, my dear, before their cats get the better of them. There is that one that would have me for dinner if I move wrongly."

She got to her knees, but no further. For some reason she'd thought he was talking about Brock, but he'd been speaking of Keith. She glanced at Viktor and Peter, who seemed to have lost their tongues. Harley looked back at his lordship, still not looking into his eyes.

"I don't know, sire. Perhaps I would not mind if they killed you. You did sentence me to this place without thought to how I would live." He nodded and smiled at her. "You are no doubt going to tell me it was for my own good?"

"It was." He turned to Viktor. "Son. I've missed you." The two of them embraced tightly and then again. Peter was suddenly brought to them as well and the three of them spoke in their own language for several minutes. She moved to stand but took a step back when his lordship reached for her.

"No; I've a mate now that will tear you apart if you touch me." He shook his head at her and pulled her to him anyway. "Damn it, sire. You've never learned to listen, have you?"

She looked at Keith and saw his cat race along his skin. Pulling away from her lord, she cleared her throat. She wasn't sure if it was the hug or the fact that Keith had become so upset over it. She turned to the room.

"This is his lordship Achard Ravengric, son of Touck Achard Ravengric, father to Viktor and Dakamon Ravengric, founder of the realm Ravengric and reigning king, if things we've just witnessed are true." He nodded at her before stepping to Ryland. "This is male to this streak Ryland Golden, son of Sandra Golden, and mate to Bronwyn Golden. His brothers and their wives respectively, Alistair and Ally Golden, Neal and Rayne Golden, Brock and Em Golden, Jules and Lenny Golden, and my mate Keith Golden."

He put out his hand to shake theirs, and Harley stepped between them. "Not without their permission. You want to connect with them, you ask first. If they don't give it freely, I will hurt you. I'm no longer your subject. I'm my own person."

He stared at her for several seconds before answering her. "Very well. But as you know I've already got one with you and then your mate. It's how I knew to come here in the first place to find you. Since you've marked him as your own...well, you know that he belongs to me now as well."

"We no longer answer to you nor the kingdom. You banished me. And now...." She looked at Keith when he cleared his throat. "He's not going to rule me. Nor you. I can't...won't...go back to that realm again."

"And you won't, either." Viktor looked at his father as he continued. "Father, just why are you here? Is what we heard true, you've really taken the throne from Dakamon?" Achard nodded and she could feel his sadness, and so apparently had Viktor. "What has he done now?"

Achard looked at her and then at the Goldens before answering. "She is of a mind that I seek your permission before we touch, as it will give us a connection much like the one you have with each other. I won't be able to hear your private conversations with your mates, but I can contact you. If you decline, I would understand."

He put out his hand, and Keith took it first. After that, each of them shook hands with him before he turned back to her. She nodded. He sat down and smiled around the room before speaking.

"Dakamon is wanted for the murder of Olivia, as well as four of his brothers. I believe he comes here now to kill Viktor as well as you, my dear." Achard leaned forward in his chair. "I should like to have you hunt him down before it comes to that."

Chapter 7

"What the hell was that man doing coming in here beating up on an old man for? I didn't do squat to him and he knocked me on my butt sure as I'm sitting here." Alistair handed Troy a baggie full of ice while they waited for the doctor to come. "He said he wanted to talk to me and when I told him I was busy, he shoved me out of the way and barged right in here as if he owned the place. Took off when Sheppard came running, didn't he, my good man?"

"He did, sire. I had never met a more rude man in all my days, Mr. Golden. He kept saying he was just here for an appointment. I've never made him any such thing, and he'll never get one now."

Sheppard, the butler, nodded as if to be making his point all the more, and Alistair took a deep breath as he leaned over the elderly man. He had a scent now and stood up to see that Troy was eyeing him closely. The man smiled. He really liked this man and his son, and hated that anything happened to him on his watch.

"Sniffing me up, are you? Good. Get his smell from my coat there. He was all over it." Alistair took it from him and put it to his nose. He couldn't believe how much it smelled of the dead man from the hospital. "You said you'd look into the letters from that other man. Alfredo Hansen was his name. Never heard a more crooked-sounding name in my life."

"He's not exactly what I'd call 'on the level.'" Alistair sat down as he watched his dear friend. "He's buying up the buildings downtown. I've been doing some searching and I found that a few years ago there was this project that was in the works that was supposed to make the area more...I guess more friendly and bring more business downtown. It was trashed along with a few other projects, and Ryland and the family went together and bought up the buildings that were no longer slated for destruction. I think we were able to get a good deal too, as the city nearly lost their shirts over the deal."

"Of course you did. What sort of business man would you be if you didn't? You think he wants to buy my two buildings in the event that the project gets off the ground again?" Alistair told him he had no idea, but he thought it might be that. "He did say something about someone wanting to have a conversation with me, as Sheppard said. I didn't get the name, and now that you say all this, he did say something about corporations and profits."

"I'll have to have a look. Did you catch your attacker's name, by the way?" Troy reached into his jacket pocket and handed him a business card. "You do know that this would have been a good deal more helpful earlier."

"What fun would that have been?" Troy sat back in his chair and tossed the bag of ice to the trash can that was more than likely older than both of them together. "I can tell you this. The man had a hard-on to get me to listen to him."

Alistair tried to think what the man that had come here had to do with the man at the hospital. And what did Troy have that needed a face to face with someone? Then he remembered something that Ryland had said.

"You bought that building downtown when Ryland told you to, right?" Troy nodded, and both of them looked up when Marcus entered the room with the doctor. He wanted to talk to both men, but waited for the doctor to look Troy over. Troy fussed loudly when the doctor suggested he go in for x-rays.

"He hit me in the hardest part of my head. What the hell will you shooting me up full of them gamma rays—or whatever they're called—do for my hard head? I'm fine. If it'll make you feel better, I'll go and have one of them done in the morning if I feel worse." Everyone in the room knew he'd not go even if he was bleeding to death.

After the doctor left, Alistair told him what he thought. "I think he's going after you because you and our firm are the only ones with property in that area that hadn't been bought by him. He's bought up the rest, and now that he's getting nothing from us...." Alistair stopped talking and looked at the men without seeing them. He reached for Keith.

Do you remember anything about that night you were run off the road? Did you get a look at the car or anything? He told him he hadn't. *But Harley did, right? Do you think I could have a conversation with her?*

She's not here. Something about going to collect her things from a locker room. She took Em and Rayne with her. I wanted to go with her but she said that she'd move faster without me. Alistair felt his frustration. *The woman is driving me nuts with keeping her distance. Do you think there will be a time when she doesn't do that?*

When this is settled, I'm sure she'll be less distracted. I need to talk to her. I don't know how to reach her but through you. Do you think you could have her come to the Cook's house when she's finished? She might know something to help out. Keith told him he'd try. *Oh, and ask her what she can do with a scent. I have one, but maybe she can track it better.*

Within two minutes, Harley was standing in the room with them. Troy nearly fell out of his chair and Marcus burst out laughing. He said he'd heard of the girl but not seen her as yet.

"You're everything Keith said you are. Lovely and a good deal stronger those other two, and I'm betting that just burns Bronwyn up, doesn't it?" Troy put out his hand to take hers. "I'd very much like a connection with you. I know that someday it might come in handy."

"It will give us a connection, more than you might have with your son. And yeah, it puts her panties in a twist all right. I love it." Troy nodded at her and left his hand out. "I don't want you to think that we are friends because of this. Being friendly with me...now at least...is very dangerous. I'm a loner, as you humans call it."

"I would never dream of thinking of us as friends." Alistair could see the gleam in the older man's eyes and hear the small laugh. "We'll just be two people who can watch out for each other. That okay with you then?"

She continued to stare at him and finally took his hand. Alistair had a moment when he thought the two of them glowed, but almost as soon as it appeared, it was gone. He looked at Marcus when he stood up and put out his hand as well.

"We've not met either. I'm thinking it would be a good thing to have you in my corner." Harley took his hand, then leaned in and frowned as she sniffed Troy. As soon as she looked at him, Alistair knew she had an idea who it was that hurt the man. She turned to look at him.

"You've met the man who's responsible for Keith being harmed?" Alistair told her he'd hurt Troy. "He is a man without scruples, and he will kill without much provocation, I think. Do you know why he was here?" Alistair shook his head. "May I help you?"

"I would appreciate it." She leaned further into Troy and sniffed hard. When she looked at him, he knew that whatever she asked of him next was going to get him and her into deep shit. "May I taste him?"

Troy looked at him, then back at her. He couldn't answer that, and he was pretty sure she knew it. When the room seemed to expand then tighten, he was startled to see Keith standing there. He wasn't sure who was more surprised by it, him or his brother.

"What the hell...?" Keith sat down and put his head between his knees as he spoke. "I was sitting in my new office thinking about...I was thinking, and I had this overwhelming need to see Harley, and then I was here. I don't think I'm supposed to do that. Am I?"

"You're my mate. Of course you can." Harley looked at him again. "May I taste him? It will go a long way to finding out what is happening here."

Keith stood up and growled low. Alistair didn't move, and neither did the other two men in the room. Harley looked at her mate, then around the room as if she didn't have a clue what was going on. It wasn't until Keith touched her that she looked like she finally got it.

"He is a male and you're jealous that he needs to touch me." Keith stood up taller and nodded. "But, seriously, I've no wish to sleep with him, only you. I only wish to help see why he was attacked. There is nothing romantic between us."

"Can you do it without licking him?" Alistair nearly laughed when she rolled her eyes at Keith. "I'm not too…why do I have this connection to Marcus too? Please tell me you didn't lick him as well. I don't want to have to kill anyone tonight."

"*I did not. He wasn't hurt.*" Harley looked at him, and Alistair could see the frustration on her face. "Explain to him what has happened so that we can resolve this without bloodshed."

"I'm not sure it will do any good, but I'll try." Harley nodded, and Alistair told Keith what was going on. "He's part of what happened to you, we think. If she can make a connection to Troy, perhaps we can track down the man responsible for your being hurt. And for some reason, she thinks that tasting him will tell her what the man wanted."

"I don't like this." Alistair didn't point out that he could tell, but waited on Keith to say something so that he could either call in a cleanup crew after he killed someone or his team to see if they could help him follow up on whatever Harley told them. He reached for his own mate when his brother pulled Harley into his arms.

There might be a chance that Harley could help us with this business we're in. She can do more things than we first thought. She asked him what. *I think she's able to find people with a touch. Something like she did with Dakamon, or whatever the hell his name is.*

An empath, you mean? There are lots of those in the world. What makes you think she is so different? He wasn't sure and told her so. *Okay then, tell me what makes you think she's able to give us this information when all our resources couldn't find shit?*

She wants to lick a wound on Troy's head to see what the man who put it there wants from him. She believes that with his blood she can find out who hurt Keith the night she saved him. Alistair felt Ally's hesitation and could understand it. *Additionally, she said that she can figure out what else he's been up to and might have planned. Can you come here now? Also, and this is pretty wonderful, Keith has the same ability to move through space that she can. I just saw him do it.*

You mean like Peter can? He told her yes. *Then I'd very much like it if you offered her a job. And him too if he'll take it. With his computer skills as well as the ability to move, we would be able to get more cases solved than we have before. Especially some of the missing children cases we've been asked to look into. The realm said to hire who we needed, right?*

I'll ask them as soon as she gets this thing taken care of. I wonder...do you suppose she's able to do much more stuff and that Keith can as well? Ally said she had no idea but was pretty sure that they'd find out soon enough.

Alistair looked at the couple before him and knew the moment that Keith agreed. As soon as he stepped back, Harley leaned into Troy and ran her tongue over the wound. As he watched, the large gash sealed up, and blood was the only thing that was there to even hint at a cut. She sat down, but Alistair had a feeling it wasn't because of the taste of the blood when suddenly he was flooded with the need to feed. He glanced at the girl and knew it was coming from her. She had to feed? When she started talking, he forgot about it.

"He works for a man named Alfredo Hansen, and was sent here to ask the man for a meeting. But he is a rogue and doesn't follow rules when they are so easily broken, and decided to get things finished for his boss." Harley looked at him as she continued. "You have met him before, this Hansen man. He knows who you are because of your dealings with the downtown project. Hansen seems to think that you're going to sell to him or else."

"Or else, huh? Not fucking likely. But why the Cooks? Is it because of the fact that they own a few of the buildings downtown as well?" She nodded, then shook her head. Alistair knew it wasn't going to be as simple as he'd hoped.

"The man that attacked this one is the driver of the car that hit the limo the night I found Keith. He was to knock it off the road and then go to check to make sure all were dead before leaving. There were to be no survivors, and if there were, he was to take care of them before leaving. I'm pretty sure he would have killed Keith had he come down the hill to the wreckage. But he's lazy and left the job to another man, who ended up not coming down either. The man that I killed in the hospital, he was with him that night. But this Mr. Brooks guy, his job was to speak to him and not cause harm. I think that there will be hell to pay when he meets up with Hansen later."

"So this Hansen sent him here to make an appointment to talk about the buildings. To what? See if he'd sell them to him?" She nodded, then looked at Keith. There was something there that he knew he needed to know, but she was clearing it with Keith first. When he nodded, she looked at him.

"He wished to kill one of the Goldens—Keith as a matter of fact—so that in his grief, Ryland would sell him the buildings that he wanted. Also, the mayor of the town is a part of what is going on, though I don't think he's a willing part." Alistair started to tell her that couldn't be possible, that the man was a loyal tiger too, but she continued before he could. "In the next several days, this man, Brooks, Carson Brooks, is to kill the mayor and make it look like an accident. His family is also being held to keep him in line until then. But what he doesn't know is that they are dead, killed the same day that they were taken from him as hostages. Brooks is not, as I said, a nice person."

All Alistair could think of was that the mayor, Carl, was going to be devastated as soon as someone told him, because he knew without a doubt that the man would be saved. Troy spoke again before Alistair could formulate a plan. The man looked like he could take on a large bear singlehandedly and come out on top.

"I want in on whatever you have going through that head of yours. If you don't agree, then I'll see him just to spite you." Alistair shook his head, but Troy kept going as if he had agreed. "I think setting up a meeting with the prick is the best way. I can act the old injured man as well as the next one. When do we start?"

Alistair knew when he wasn't going to win and only nodded, but he'd find a way to keep the man on the lower end of whatever they did. "We'll have to wait until we have enough information on the project before we can proceed. And Ryland will have to approve. But I want to go on record as saying this is a bad idea."

"Duly noted," Marcus said to him. As Alistair reached for Ryland, something else occurred to him. In less than forty-eight hours, the king of Ravengric was coming, and now this shit. He wondered if his life would ever be normal. Then he thought of all the fun he'd be missing out on.

We have a problem here. Can you come to the Cooks' house?

~~~

Dakamon hated the fact that the sun drained him so much. In his own world things like this simply didn't happen because he deemed it so. This world was a disappointment all the way around, especially when it came to getting someone

93

to help him in his daily dress. There just were not enough servants here.

He'd not dressed or undressed himself in nearly a thousand years. The thought of having to do so now had confused as well as frustrated him. He'd never had to make a button work or tie his own shoes, much less purchase them. He was glad now that he'd found the woman, Cindy, that was doing it for him, because those first two mornings had been a nightmare.

"You'll be wanting no dinner, I'm guessing." Dakamon didn't answer her when she leaned over him to wipe a smudge off his shoe. "There is plenty of food in the house, yet you don't eat nary a bite. What do I do with it if not to feed you?"

He wanted to tell her to find him a girl he could fuck and drink from and use the offending food to fatten her up so she'd live through it, but continued to keep his mouth shut. His fangs had dropped in his hunger, and he doubted very much the old woman would bare her throat if he asked her to.

"I should like for you to find more help for the house. I will require a staff of about…." He realized he had no idea how many ran his castle at home and told her the first number that popped into his head. "Fifty should be enough to keep this house in order."

She snorted. "Fifty would be enough, all right, if you have the money to pay them. I'm still waiting for my first check to come through. You pay up and I'll see what I can do about getting you a staff."

Dakamon pulled out the wad of cash he'd had stashed in this realm in the event something might happen. He had no idea how much was enough, or for that matter how the numbering system worked on the bills. He had a clue that the higher the numbers on something the more it had to be worth, and handed her a bill with three numbers. A lesson in the cash system, he thought, was in order.

"Five hundred is a good start." He handed her two more with the same markings on it. "I'll get you a staff, but it might cost you more than this. People don't like to do domestic like they used to."

He knew neither what a domestic was nor what their job might consist of. All he knew for sure was that he had to feed soon or he was going to be in big trouble. He licked his lips at the thought of taking someone to his bed and having his way with them as he drained them. As soon as she left him in his room, he went to the smallish room that held what he supposed was an office.

The computer, as he'd heard Cindy call it, was something that he'd seen working but had never used. There were people to do that for him. He'd played with it over the past few days, but was no closer to figuring it out than he'd been before. The machine simply made no sense. Dakamon reached for his brother, thinking to needle him a bit more to see what he knew about Harley. It was something he could do while he got his body to calm.

So you've gone and gotten yourself banished from Ravengric. Dakamon didn't like that he knew about his recent problems, but it appeared that his brother knew a good deal more. *And you thought to take care of me as well when you came in on the guise of business. Where are you staying, my dear brother?*

I did nothing wrong, and as soon as I can get my hands on that girl, I'll be back where I need to be. She's spreading lies and no doubt her legs to anyone who has the coin. Dakamon flushed when he realized his brother was laughing at him. *She's a murdering bitch. And as soon as I can make her confess to killing your mate, I'll be sitting on the throne.*

You're not going to get a confession from her and we both know it. You'll be lucky if she lets you say anything once she's found you, much less lets you accuse her of something that we both know now she didn't do. His brother's voice was calm, much too calm for him to think he didn't know more than he was saying. *Then there are the other people, the ones you murdered or had murdered in the name of you being king. How many servants have you killed for your own pleasure, Dakamon? How many have died to make sure you're satisfied? Is that all you thought being king was?*

Those damned servants again. When was he going to be able to do what he wanted without his family breathing down his neck all the time? He thought about what his father had said to him and wondered if he'd contacted Viktor yet. More than likely not. There was no way his father would leave the kingdom unattended. Not to mention his father would not just come to this world without contacting someone, and he knew his brother well enough to know that he'd have announced that bit of information right away.

I'm only here on a leave. I needed to get away and without all the fanfare that goes with my traveling. As for the others, I've no idea what you're talking about. Where is the girl? I've told you several times now that she is to come to me. Are you disobeying a direct order from your king? While Dakamon waited for his brother to tell him he was bringing her to him, he tried to think where he could meet him. The kingdom was out of the question, of course, but there had to be —

As you are no longer king, I no longer have to bow before you, and your word has no meaning to me. Not that it has for many years. And as for the girl, Harley won't be coming to you either unless it's to bring you before the king. Father was most insistent in finding where you have gotten yourself. He felt his brother's laughter. *I believe she'd bring you in for no payment at all.*

He's paying her? To find me? Dakamon sat up straighter in his chair and tried to think what his father had been...then something else occurred to him. *Where is Father now?*

Sitting beside me. We've had a lovely reunion today. He said to tell you hello and that your days are numbered. The laughter again had him curling into himself. *Harley said to tell you that she's coming for you. And that when she finds you, the beating you gave her will be nothing compared to what she does to you. And Dakamon?*

Dakamon felt his skin crawl at the sound of his brother's voice, suddenly so cold and hard. *Yes Viktor, what is it now?* The bravado he tried to put into his voice was fake, and he was sure they both knew it.

If I find you before she does, then you'd better hope that you can end your miserable life before I do. Because if you don't, I'm going to make you suffer in ways you won't be able to imagine.

The connection was broken off, and Dakamon sat there for several minutes just waiting for him to come into the room and do just what he'd said he would. Viktor knew that he'd killed his mate, and Dakamon had no doubt that he'd find many painful ways to get the job done. Dakamon had a moment when he wished that he could find Harley now so that he could be spared whatever it was that Viktor was thinking. The girl had been a guardian for many, many years before being brought here, and even though she had had no use for her powers here, she would still be able to track him if his father asked her to and to use her magic. When nothing happened, he began to relax a little. Maybe his brother had no knowledge of where Harley was and his father was still in Ravengric.

"That's what it is. Viktor is just guessing about things. There is no way he has anything on me. If he did, I'd be a hunted man, and I'm not that." Dakamon looked around the room again just to be sure, then laughed at himself. "You've become quite paranoid in your olden years, my good man. Just relax."

He heard someone coming down the hall seconds before the door was knocked on. He didn't bother getting up but allowed the person to enter. The woman standing there nearly took his breath away.

"I am here for the job interview." She looked around the room and smiled at him, and Dakamon felt his cock fill. "Where would you like me?"

He knew that he shouldn't touch her, but he could smell her freshness all the way across the room. Crooking his finger at her, she smiled again and moved toward him. He stood up when she was within touching distance. Lifting her chin up, he looked her in the eyes and snared her. She was his now.

"Take off your clothes." Nodding, she removed her blouse, then her bra. He watched her, mesmerized, as she stripped down to nothing. Having her lean over the chair with her ass up, he moved up behind her and freed his cock. He didn't bother seeing if she was ready for him as he slammed into her. As soon as he sank his fangs into her throat and drank greedily, he knew that she'd never survive him, so he took all he wanted as he fucked her until she bled. Dakamon could feel the life giving blood revive him.

Chapter 8

Keith was standing at the door when she came up the stairs. He could see that she was exhausted, but more than that, he could see that she had been crying as well. For some reason that upset him more than anything else that had happened today. Who dared make his mate cry?

"We have located the king, somewhat. And the man who attacked Mr. Cook has been found as well. He will be watched by your brother Brock and his mate." She yawned when she leaned against the railing. "I have worked hard today and my body is spent."

Keith went to her slowly and picked her up. He knew she was tired when she said nothing. When she leaned her head on his shoulder, he felt his tiger purr and he knew she felt it. The look in her eyes made him want to shift and take her.

"Your tiger wants to play." He nodded at her. "I would like that as well. Do you think that we could go into the woods and run? I think it would go a long way to helping me relax."

"You can shift?" She nodded. "Into a cat or anything you wish?" She nodded again, and he found he either had to sit her down on her feet or drop her. When she lifted her arms above her head, he watched as her cat took her. It was slow and sexy, and Keith had the urge to rub his body all over her.

She is not my favorite animal, but she could become that. Harley moved around his legs, weaving in and out of them as she continued. *I can shift to anything I need to, including things that aren't living. As a guardian it was sometimes necessary to shift to hide in plain sight.*

You're very beautiful. He heard her purr and dropped down to his knees before her as she marked every part of him. *You can shift with your clothes on?*

Yes, as can you, but I love to watch you strip. I can't be naked when I'm watching someone, silly. It would be…distracting, I think. He smiled. *You're still a human, Keith. Don't you want to come play with me? I can do it myself, I suppose, but it's so much more fun when you're with me.*

Standing, he went to the lower level of the house with her right beside him. He wanted to run with her more than anything, but the cook had left for the day and someone had to open the door. As soon as she ran out the door and settled on the deck to wait for him, he shut the door and came out. When he reached for his buttons on his shirt, she stopped him.

I can't wait for you this time. I need you to be a cat so we can play. There is no difference in how you shift other than you no longer have to take off your clothes. He felt her arousal. *Unless, of course, you'd like for me to shift back and we skip playing and simply fuck here.*

I don't know how long I can wait for you. He felt his cat snarl at him to get with it. *I want to fuck you this way and as a tiger. The thought of taking you and marking you has my tiger close to the surface.*

Let him come. She stood up and looked out at the woods. He felt her tense. Then she suddenly relaxed. *There is a wolf in the woods. He is there by invitation from you. Should I chase him off while you think about coming to play?*

The teasing tone in her voice had him shift quickly. He looked for her, only to see a streak of gold disappear into the woods. As soon as he crossed into the dark forest, he could smell the wolf. It was his friend and cop, Jimmy Cole. As he came out of the woods in front of him, the wolf laughed. As they had formed a blood bond long ago, they could speak to each other.

She's running me off. Told me that I had to chase my tail elsewhere tonight. Jimmy laughed. *She's a beautiful cat by the way. Is she your mate?*

She is. Keith saw her just as Jimmy told him good luck. Keith watched for her only to wonder if she'd shifted to something else. When she ran in front of him, Keith knew that there would be nothing he ever saw again that would match her beauty. He took off after her and laughed when she darted away.

They chased each other for nearly an hour. Her exhaustion seemed to fade away with every passing moment. When he finally found her lying beside a cave, he moved to stand over her and looked around the deepening darkness.

Close your eyes. He did as she said. *Feel the forest around you? There are many things you can feed from here. The animals and the earth are there as well, but you can feed from anything surrounding you. Shifters will give you the most, but you must be careful not to drain them.*

Feed from them? I don't understand. I don't need to feed, do I? He felt her energy as it started to fade a little, then a little more. *Harley, will I need to feed like a vampire does?*

If you wish, you can. I need to feed to survive, but not as often if I can come out here to feed from the earth. But if my energy is too low, this will only give me enough to survive; but sometimes that isn't enough. He could hear her voice fade and wondered about it until she spoke. *I'll not bite you again unless you want it. I can feed from others if necessary.*

Keith tried to remember if she'd ever fed from him since that first time she'd bitten him, and she hadn't. He wondered if her exhaustion had anything to do with that, and he felt a small touch to his mind.

Where is Harley? Peter sounded panicky, and that made Keith nervous. *She is not well. And I cannot reach her.*

Not well how? When he didn't answer, Keith shifted and went to Harley. She was sleeping, but very deeply. When he shook her to wake her, she moaned but didn't open her eyes. He was suddenly very, very afraid. *Peter, does she have to drink blood daily?*

Not daily because of her age, but she needs it at least weekly. Has she drunk from you, Keith? He told him she hadn't. *You must wake her and give her your vein. She is very weak. Too weak, I'm thinking now.*

Keith lifted her up and cradled her into his arms. Saying her name over and over wasn't working, so he moved into her mind and commanded her to wake. Her tiger growled at him. Then she shifted. He was startled by how pale she was.

Think of biting her, and your fangs will drop. Keith tried not to think about having fangs right now, but did as Peter had asked. When he felt them burst through his gums, he bit into his own wrist. *Be careful that she doesn't drink too deeply from you. You're not as old as she is, and she may harm you.*

As soon as his wrist touched her mouth, she moaned. He rubbed his blood over her lips and felt his cock jerk in his pants when she moaned again. Christ, I'm a pervert, he thought, to have these sort of feeling for a woman who was starving for his blood. When her mouth covered his wound, he pulled her closer to him until she was nearly in his lap.

Her fingers curling around his forearm to hold him had him looking into her eyes.

"That's it, baby. Drink all you need." Keith shifted her twice over his hard cock, trying to find some relief, before she finally lifted her head. Breathing hard, he stared at her as his blood stained her mouth.

"You fed me." He nodded, not sure what to say to her. "Do you know what your blood does for me? Do you have any idea what your taste makes me feel?"

"Hunger." She nodded and pressed her mouth to his. Keith ate at her mouth, drinking in her essences as she pushed him back to the ground. When she was over him, he held onto her hips while she rode him. "I need you. Right now, I need you."

"Yes," she hissed at him. His clothes were suddenly gone, as were hers. As soon as she sat up on her knees, he helped her guide herself over him. When she lowered herself onto him, Keith lay very still as she moved back and forth. He felt her pleasure, wore it as though it were his. Sitting up, he took her nipple into his mouth and suckled hard. Her hips moved quicker, harder over him until he couldn't take it any longer and rolled her to her back as he licked her throat.

This time when he felt his fangs drop, there was no pain, only the most incredible need to mark her. When she tilted her neck, giving him what he didn't even know he wanted, he licked the pounding pulse and then gently sank them into her.

~~~

"Keith," she screamed at her body detonated. Every cell in her body seemed to feel it. The climax didn't just take her, it tore her apart into particles only to come back together again more alive than she'd ever felt. When he suckled the first time, pulling her blood from her into him, the connection that was there before seemed to snap around them, until there was nothing but them, one soul, one mind, and one love. Keith lifted his head and stilled above her.

"You're mine." She nodded at him. "I love you. More than I've ever dreamed...no, more than I've ever known a person could love another."

"You are mine as well. And I will love you now and forever. We are one, as you said." Wrapping her legs around him, she moaned when he moved deeper. "Come with me, Keith. Please? Come with me."

When he began to move again, his cock slipping in and out of her, he moved slowly, with care and love. Never did he stop looking at her, staring deeply into her eyes as if he were looking deeply into her soul. When she pulled him to her mouth, he came willingly and kissed her with a gentleness that took her breath away.

This time when she came, she bowed her back and let it take her, much in the same way her animals did, and felt the need to mark him again. Taking his throat, she drank from him, leaving a scar on his flesh for all to see. When Keith came with her, his body bowing back, the roar that spilled from his mouth made her skin pebble and her hair dance. Harley was in love with this man.

When he dropped over her, she welcomed the weight. Rolling to his back, he took her with him and she spread her body over his like a blanket and laid her head on his chest to hear his pounding heart. As his heart slowed to a normal rhythm, she smiled and lifted her head to look at him.

"You are an amazing lover." He grinned at her and she laughed. "Don't let it go to your head. I was merely letting you know that I was satisfied."

"Well of course you were. I am Keith Golden." She slapped at him and laughed. She laid her head back on his chest to listen to his heart beat out a smooth rhythm for her. Soon she was dozing and the sound of his voice startled her a little. "Why didn't you tell me you needed blood to survive?"

She didn't want to lie to him, wasn't even sure she could, so she sat up and looked down at him. This was going to be hard and she didn't want to upset him after what they'd just shared. Looking out into the dark woods, she thought about her answer before speaking.

"I have been alone for so many years, getting by with only what I needed. Sometimes it would be years before I would speak to someone with words, other than what I needed to work. I would feed weekly, and only then if I could find someone that was less than...most of my prey were homeless people who had no idea what I was or what I needed from them. It was...I suppose that it was my intention to continue on the same way. I didn't want to ask you for something that you might not want to give. I didn't want you to tell me no, or worse, be sickened by me."

"Sickened by you? Not at all possible. Did you think I'd turn you down, really?" He was saddened and hurt when she nodded at him. "I would never have denied you anything, especially something as vital to you as blood. Please take what you need from me."

"I will need to now. From you I mean. I will not go back to...I cannot go back to starving again and being alone. I don't...I don't think I could." He pulled her back to his body, and she lay there, feeling the tears fall. "Why are you so good to me? I am not the kind of person that you would normally be with, am I?"

"I don't know what you mean by that. I'm nice to you because I love you. As for you not being the kind of person I'm normally with, that's only true because I've never been with my mate before. You are my world and I want to make you happy." He rolled her to her back as he continued. "We never got to run as tigers. My tiger was so ready to mount you and mark you. He's very jealous."

Harley let her tiger take her, and she laughed when Keith scrambled back. As soon as he shifted as well, she could feel his need. When he commanded her to run, she took off without a thought to why she was doing as he bid when she wanted to fight everyone else when they tried to order her about. But with Keith it was different.

Lying close to the ground so he'd have to search for her, she thought about her life here not so very long ago. It had taken her decades to get over her bitterness at being sent here, and more than another one to try to figure out how to live. She had all her magic, but it did her little good when things in this world were so different than the one she'd come from. The world was nothing compared to what it was now. Not even the people were the same. But life had been easier for her here.

In Ravengric she'd been assigned daily duties, most of which consisted of finding pleasure whores for the king. Not that she minded the real work, but working for him had been a trial. Dakamon had never been a good child and had been a terrible teenager. But he really began to make his mark when he became an adult, and not in a good way. He'd been cruel and heartless, killing without thought to how it would affect those left behind. She'd had to go to families' homes more and more the older he got to inform them of their child's death, all in the name of the king. Money poured from the coffers as if there were an endless supply of it. She supposed that it did for Dakamon, who had never been held accountable for anything. Until now.

Keith moved in front of her and just when she thought he was going to move past, he leapt at her, startling her so much that she forgot to run. When he took her to the ground she snarled at him, but was truly caught before she could do much more than that. When he sank his teeth into her shoulder, she snarled again but was ready for him.

Christ, he needs you. She moaned to Keith in agreement. *He's not going to be as gentle as I would be.*

Take me. He mounted her hard and quick. His cock filled her, and she knew that this was going to be more of a marking than anything else. When he began to piston into her, she moved back to take him deeper, only to have him tear deeper into her muscle. Harley wasn't gentle either. Her cat was just as aggressive as his was, and they seemed to be enjoying it. As soon as he tore his mark into her flesh, Harley roared out her release. Keith's cat followed her with his own.

They shifted as one. Keith slammed his cock into her hard and fast, as if he had not taken her only moments before. When he took her mouth, it, too, felt as if he was desperate for her, and she met him stroke for stroke until he threw back his head and shouted out her name. Harley's own release was just as complete. Sated, she felt her eyes drift close, even as Keith dropped his weight on top of her. Willing them to their bed, she felt his small laughter and then nothing more.

Harley opened her eyes quickly, not even sure what had awakened her. Reaching for Keith, she found him sleeping beneath her and all was well with him. Reaching out into the room, she found nothing more than a fly on the lamp by the door and a small spider racing across the room toward the window that was left open. It took her a few minutes, but she found the being on the front deck standing by the door. Waiting before she touched his mind, she was startled to find the king there.

You are well then? She told him she was. *I would like a word with you, if you please? There is...Dakamon had been found, but he has killed again. A human this time. The world cannot know of our kind.*

I will be down momentarily. I cannot invite you in, as this is not my home. I only live here with Keith. She felt his laughter at her statement. *I do not presume anything, my lord. He has neither given me leave to call this home, nor has he said that he gives me anything. I am his mate but nothing more. He has said that he loves me and I him, but that does not make his home mine.*

I believe you are much more to him than even that, and you well know it, child. His laughter again made her feel out of sorts, but he continued before she could comment. *I shall wait here then. Please wake your mate. I believe he will be most displeased with me should he find you on the porch with me even before the sun rises.*

When she lifted her head, Keith looked at her. He didn't ask but got up to dress too. As she had nothing here, he handed her a shirt of his and a pair of soft cotton pants. She had to cinch them tight to keep them up. He grinned at her all the way down the stairs. She decided that she was going to make him pay if it was the last thing she did.

Harley wasn't surprised to see both Peter and Ryland there as well.

"I hope you have something to eat here. This bastard woke me before I could even grab a banana." Ryland moved into the kitchen and took three apples and two peaches out of the bowl before sitting down. Then he hopped up again to grab a glass of tea as well as some cheese.

"Make yourself at home, big brother." Keith handed him a plate as well as a napkin as he continued. "From your scowl I'm guessing this is not a social call."

"Dakamon has killed a human. No one knows who has murdered the young woman, but I have seen enough of my son's work to know the signs. He must be stopped." Keith went out of the room, leaving her with the men only to return a few minutes later with a laptop and two other devices that he laid on the table between her and Ryland. The king looked at his equipment with a smile. "You can find him on that?"

"I can. In fact, with the information that Viktor and Harley gave me yesterday, I was able to pinpoint about where he may have bought a house. There are three that were purchased in the area that paid with cash." Harley watched as he pulled up each one and knew the moment she saw the third one that it belonged to Dakamon.

"It is that one." Keith looked at her and nodded, not even questioning how she might know. But the need to explain was deeply ingrained in her head. "He would want a house that was large and that would make a statement. Dakamon was nothing but a man who would want the world, either world, to know that he was here and he had riches. And it looks on the scale of the one I saw yesterday." She flushed and started to apologize to the king.

"No, you're right, my dear. He would want the biggest and the best, no matter whether he needed it or not. Yes, I believe you are correct." The king winked at her, and she was suddenly overwhelmed with embarrassment. "Viktor said you'd be the one to find him. I guess he was correct."

"She will need to go to him. He must be stopped." Peter nodded at his own statement. "Soon too, for he will not be long for wanting another kill. There was a time when I actually believed him to be a good man. I cannot believe how far he has fallen. Well, not really, I suppose, but just recently so that I've noticed. "

"You think he kills for the pleasure of it?" Everyone looked at Ryland when he asked. "I mean, I understand that you need to drink blood to survive, but to kill without justification? Is there a law like that in your world? Because there certainly is here."

"There is, but as he had the entire castle in fear of him, I did not find out about his fetish until recently. It is with great shame that I admit that I have been a failure to the kingdom."

Harley shook her head at her king and spoke to him as she would any of the Golden men.

"You trusted a man who should have been trustworthy beyond all others." Harley dropped her head when she realized she'd spoken to the king without his permission. He lifted her chin up and looked into her eyes.

"You must never feel like this again, Harley. You've been hurt more than anyone in all of this because of me and my not looking into the deaths sooner. Had I done something, Viktor's Olivia might still be with us, there would not be so many dead in our villages, and you would have been home with your family." He nodded to her as if that was enough. And she supposed that it was to him. "Of course there would be no mate for Keith, and for that I'm eternally grateful, as I'm sure he is."

"I am," Keith told him as he held her. "I'm happier to have her in my life than I've ever dreamed I'd be. And more in love with her than I'd ever thought I'd be with one person."

The plans were set into motion to go to the former king and take him back to Ravengric to stand trial. Not that there was much of a need for a trial. Much like when she'd been found guilty of killing Olivia, it only needed the king's approval for him to face his sentencing as well as having it carried out. Killing a human in this world was certain death. Dakamon was going to be beheaded as soon as he was found guilty.

Chapter 9

"I don't understand. You're telling me that the one person I wanted you to kill is now not only healthy, but he's up and about as if nothing happened to him? How is that even possible? The last I had heard he was fighting to live from a horrific accident that you caused." Carson didn't say anything but nodded. Alfredo shook his head as he continued. "No, there is no sitting there as if you have it all figured out and thinking that you nodding like a fucking dog in the back of a car is going to satisfy me. Tell me what happened, starting with Golden and ending with how one of your men was killed during a simple clean-up job."

"You want I should start from where I was or from where my brother was?" Alfredo only stared at the man. Who the hell talked like that? He told him to start wherever. "Well, I was at the Cooks' house. Did you know that they have a butler? He is a strong motherfucker too. As soon as I came in the door, like he was all over my shit."

"And that made it so that you couldn't make an appointment for me to see him how? And if you tell me that you only roughed him up again, I will pull out my gun and shoot you on principle. Get to the point." Alfredo could feel another headache coming on and it wasn't even ten in the morning yet. "What happened at the Cooks' house? And don't think this will get you out of telling me what happened at the hospital."

"I went there and knocked on the door like I thought I should have." Alfredo reached into his top drawer, pulled out the gun, and sat it on the desk. "I'm getting there. I'm getting there. I went to the house and knocked, but Cook was coming up the drive so I waited. The big man, the butler, opened the door and kinda scared me a little. When Cook came up on the front steps, I was a little jumpy and I tried to explain why I was there. Suddenly he was all defensive like and I had to get out of there. But I did convey that you wanted a word with him and gave over that business card you gave me."

Alfredo stared at him, trying to work out in his head how the hell this man had survived all these years without someone shooting him in the head simply to shut him up. He sat back down in his chair to try and reason through what was going on. Nothing came to mind so he simply asked what he needed to know.

"So not only did you maim the man, but you left my calling card there so they'd know who to contact in the event they want to press charges." Alfredo decided that this man was much too stupid to live and actually thought of the bullet entering his head. "I don't suppose you asked him if he wanted to sell to me, did you? I don't know, maybe let him know of the plans that were going to take place where his buildings now stand?"

"Nah, I didn't tell him shit. Just tossed him to the ground, then took off. I had to run back to give him the card, but I did get on out of there when that butler came running after me. He sure is fast for a big man."

Alfredo opened his mouth to say something but closed it, not sure what he should say. Even if he could form the words, he wasn't sure Carson would get it. Rubbing his forehead, he thought of what the hell this could mean for his business when his phone rang. Picking it up without bothering with the caller ID, he answered with a bark of his name.

"Mr. Hansen? This is Marcus Cook. You sent your hood to our home a few days ago to rough up my father." The man's voice was as cool and calm as Alfredo had ever heard. "Your man said you wanted to speak to us."

"Yes. I'm dreadfully sorry about your father. Will he be all right?" Marcus told him he would. "That's good news. I'm dealing with the young man as we speak. I want you to know that I do not tolerate that sort of —"

"You didn't give a fig about my father's health then or now. Cut to the chase, would you? I have things I'd like to accomplish today." Still a calm voice, but there was a bit more bite to his voice that Alfredo found to be rude. Before he could point it out to the man, he spoke again. "If you're asking about the property again, you're wasting your breath. We've got plans for that building, and they don't include selling dirt cheap to you so you can sell it to the city for a project that is never going to see the light of day."

"Who told you about the project?" The laughter at the other end had Alfredo seeing red. "There are only a handful of people who know about that deal and I demand you tell me who told you about it." Marcus laughed again. This time his humor was apparent, as well as his sarcasm.

"Oh my, you want me to tell you who told me? Well by all means, let me simply do as you say." Yet another tone from the man, this one was hard and very unforgiving. "You can make your demands to someone who might take them seriously, but not me, you moronic idiot. I'm a very wealthy man, Hansen, and if you fuck with me and my father again, I'll make you regret the day you came from your mother's body." A finger of fear slid down Alfredo's back as Marcus continued. "I have been around a good deal longer than you, you little shit for brains. If you think you can threaten me and get away with it, you're stupider than the man you sent to kill Keith. And when the police figure it out, you're going down for four homicides. We will not sell."

So the man had connected the dots. If he had, others would too. The line went dead, but before he could hang it up, Alfredo picked up his gun and pointed it at Carson. It was time to cut his losses and get the fuck out of town. Now before it was too late.

"You're not going to shoot me, are you?" Carson sounded so humored by the thought that Alfredo simply pulled the trigger. The butler came into the room several minutes later with a gold tray in his hands that was topped with a small card.

"Tell him I'll meet him in the library." Without a word he went out. Alfredo knew he'd seen the gun, and it would be impossible for him to have missed the blood, not to mention the dead body that lay slumped in the chair across from his desk. Alfredo put his weapon in the back of his pants and moved around Carson to the door. Before he left the room, he went back to the desk and picked up the stack of money that was always laying there. He'd need that if he wanted to make a clean break.

"Ah, there you are. I'd thought you'd forgotten about me." Rocco sat in the large wing-backed chair as if he had not a care in the world. Alfredo's man was serving him a coffee.

"I had some business to take care of." He sat down to think. "How many people have you told about this project we have going?"

Rocco shifted on his seat, obviously not liking being questioned about this. "Why do you ask? I would ask you the same, you know. A great many people have a great deal of knowledge about this. Who have you told?"

"You." Rocco stared at him for several seconds before Alfredo got up to pace. The man had told enough people that it had gotten back to the Cooks and no doubt the Goldens. As of right now, the deal was as good as dead, and he was pretty sure they both knew it. He began to pace harder while thoughts of money, blood, and deal circled around his head until he couldn't make heads or tails out of what was what. So far three men had been killed, not including Carson, and he had tied up more than fifty million of his own money on buildings that were worth less than a quarter of that, and now it was all coming to shit.

"What's the progress on your venture? I've a great deal of money invested in this and—"

Alfredo cut him off. He'd had enough of this bastard too. "Who has money invested in this? You? Or do you have a bunch of your friends giving you money to invest in it for them? Because as far as I can see, you've never done anything but make it impossible for us to finish the venture, because everyone you meet you tell about it." Alfredo sat down and glared at the man who had been everything to him. "Cook called me. He said that as far as the project goes, it's dead. He won't sell, and he knows about the connection to him and the Golden man too. As much as told me to look for the cops to come knocking at my door. And I think most of that is because of you telling every fucking idiot that stands near you."

"I had nothing to do with that Golden incident. As far as that goes, you did that all on your own. Didn't you? Just say to me you did all that with the Golden boy, and I'll try my best to end this for you." Rocco was poised, waiting for an answer, and Alfredo had a feeling he had missed something. He sat up and thought about the wording of the sentence.

"Christ, you're wired, aren't you?" Rocco didn't deny it but flushed brightly. "Mother fuck. How long? How long have you been working with the cops?"

"I don't know what you're referring to." He stood up and so did Alfredo. "I'm going to go now, and you should have yourself a very lovely day."

The doors to the front of his house burst open, and before he could make his way to the back of the house where he had a way to escape, his man...the man he'd barely exchanged three words with over the course of the past five years...came in with a gun and pointed it right at him.

"Drop the weapon, Hansen, it's over." Alfredo couldn't believe this was happening. Even as the police with flak jackets and numerous initials blazed over their vests and jackets came into his house, shouting at him to stop and drop, he still could not believe that he'd been turned in by the one man he'd trusted above all others.

"Why?" Rocco didn't answer him, as he too was being cuffed and tossed to the floor as if he wasn't anything more to them than a common criminal. "Why the hell did you do this to me?"

"It was you or I, and I've no desire to spend the rest of my life being ass fucked by a bunch of lowlifes while in prison. Turning you in got me a reduced sentence, as well as a nice cell with all the comforts of home." Rocco's laughter caught him off guard. It was manic and a little loud. "I'm going to prison for nothing more than trying to better myself. What is wrong with this world, I ask you?"

"Alfredo Hansen, you are under arrest for the murder of Carson Brooks, extortion, money laundering, prostitute of a minor, and theft." Alfredo looked at his butler, who winked. "You've been a very bad boy, Hansen, and it is with the greatest pleasure that I get to be the one that tells you that it's now time to pay the piper."

"You motherfucking son of a bitch. I paid you to work for me, not spy on me." The man nodded, and that's when Alfredo realized he had no idea what his name was. "How long have you been working for the Feds?"

He knelt down to look him in the eye. Alfredo was in no position to straighten up, so the man still towered over him. With a grin that made him want to smack the shit out of him, the man finally answered him. "I've been a federal officer since you were still in diapers, and taking you down is going to make my retirement so much the sweeter."

They were dragging him out to the yard as they were bringing out the body of Carson. Carson had had it coming and he tried his best to tell them that. He begged them for one more look at his lovely body. Maybe only a look at his hands that he'd dreamed about for nights on end, thinking about them being on his body. Then Alfredo saw someone he'd never thought to see again. Keith Golden was standing by a girl who he'd never seen before.

"You should have simply learned to take no for an answer." Keith laughed as he continued. "But then if you had, I might not have met my future wife. I suppose then I should thank you for your part in all this."

Alfredo wasn't one to turn down a good thing. He was being shoved into a police car even as he tried to speak to the younger man. Finally when Keith said to let him speak, Alfredo was freed just enough to stand on his own two feet but not much else.

"Then we're all good? You can tell them you're okay with this misunderstanding and they'll let me go?" Keith shook his head. "Why not? I did you a favor, just like you said. How would you be this happy had I not tried to kill you?"

He realized his mistake the moment the words left his mouth. Another Golden was standing there and he nodded to the officers holding him. He'd just basically confessed, and even though he now wanted a lawyer, he'd done it after he'd been read his rights and before asking for an attorney. He was so fucked. Alfredo begged for his life the entire time he was being shoved into the car and even after he was locked inside. Somehow he didn't think anyone was going to save him.

~~~

Dakamon moved along the alley to find someone to feed from. As of last night he'd been unable to stay in his home due to all the law standing around it. He had no idea what he'd done here that they would know about so quickly, but he knew better than to let them take him. For whatever reason they thought they should hold him, he was sure there were a good deal more people looking for him for crimes that these humans knew nothing about. Dakamon ducked behind a building when he heard the siren shrilling.

He'd never heard such a noisy place. Not only were there cars all over the roadways, but there were so many people here that seemed to have one job in life, and that was to piss him off. And those who weren't out to make him mad? They were there to annoy others into making his life more difficult.

Then there was the problem with keeping his money. He'd never had to pay for things in his life, and he was reasonably sure that his housekeeper, as she told him to call her, was taking more than she needed. Every day it was something more for her. The water had to be paid for, as did the electricity and heat. He'd pointed out to her that he needed neither of those things, but she had only put out her hand for more money. Now he was down to nothing more than a few of the paper bills that he'd stashed here, and nothing much else. He tried to remember what she'd told him about the cash she was taking.

"You have to keep it in your wallet." He nodded at her, not having a clue what a wallet was or why one would keep it. "Then when you pull it out to use it, don't ever let anyone see the contents. They'll rob you blind."

That was another thing he disliked about this place. No one ever said what they meant. And he did not get the…what was it she called it? Oh yes, sarcasm. That was another thing he wished he could abolish. If he ran this world, that would be the first thing that he'd make gone.

"You looking for a good time, buddy?" The woman smelled of strong perfume with a hint of urine. He stepped back from her before she could touch him. "I could blow you for twenty bucks."

He assumed she meant suck his cock and thought that whatever amount twenty bucks was, he'd pay it, even if he had to hold his breath while she did it. Nodding to her, he handed her what he thought was a twenty, and she slipped it into her shirt before he could inquire if that was the right bill. Taking his hand, she led him down the alley he'd just been in.

Dropping to her knees before him, she had his trousers open and his cock out almost immediately. The moment she took him into her mouth, he leaned back against the building to watch what she was doing. She may smell badly, but she could blow him anytime she wanted. When she started to bob her head up and down over him, he curled his hand into her hair and held her while he fucked her. Christ, she was going to make him come before he could take much pleasure from it. Lifting her by her hair, he jerked her around so that her ass was in front of him and tore her clothing off.

"Hey, you didn't pay for that." She tried to struggle from him but he held her to him as he slammed his cock into her ass. Her scream had him putting his hand over her mouth as he continued to fuck her tight ass. As soon as his release was near, he lifted her throat to his mouth and tore into her vein. She didn't struggle so much as fight him for all she was worth then. But it mattered little. The more he drank from her, the weaker she became even as he came deep within her. He reached into her bra with the intent to twist her nipple to give her blood that last bit of spice of pain, but instead he found a great deal of money stuffed in there, much more than he had given her. He then searched her further, finding even more in her pockets and a small bag around her waist. Leaving her where he dropped her, Dakamon decided that he needed to find more of such women and take his pleasure, as well as whatever monies they had on them. This was the most profitable fuck he'd ever had.

By morning he had amassed a great deal of the paper money. He'd had his fill long before he'd finished with the last woman, but he'd been having such a sated night that he'd continued on for five more of them. Now he lined up the paper in matching numbers and wished again he knew what he had. But for now he was satisfied that he could find a place to rest until he could begin again. Dakamon found a house deep in the city when the sun was cresting the sky. Killing the family that resided there proved no problem for him, as he was as satisfied both sexually and with blood as he'd ever been. Leaving them where they lay, he went to the sublevels to rest.

As soon as he was lying down, he felt a small touch of his mind. Dakamon tried to ignore it, but the more he tried that the more insistent the person became until he finally let them speak to him. He didn't want his rest disturbed and thought this the only way to rid himself of them.

Hello Dakamon, have you found yourself a good place to hide as yet? His body froze at the sound of her voice; Harley continued speaking to him as if they were old friends. *I have been looking for you. Do you suppose that leaving a trail of bodies for us to find is a smart move? Especially since you knew your father had hired me to find you?*

You are not to speak to me unless I give you leave to. Don't tell me that you've forgotten the rules of our world so quickly. So I ask you, what is it you want, criminal? There can be nothing you have to say to me that – Her laughter made him sit up in the bed and look for her, as it sounded as if she were in the room with him. *I demand that you show yourself.*

Demand? You certainly demand a great deal for a person without a home or a realm. Here they call that being without a pot to piss in or a window to toss it out of. I think not, Dakamon. I no longer have to obey you. You are no longer my king. You are no longer anything to me. Dakamon wanted to argue with her, but there was nothing in what she was saying that wasn't true. *I'm hunting you.*

Terror poured over him like freezing water. He closed the connection quickly, but still worried that it was too late. She was good at what she did, very good. The fact that she'd found the body of Olivia so quickly gave testament to that. Dakamon had hidden her body very well.

He'd killed her. Dakamon would not admit that to anyone but himself, but felt now that it was too late even for that. They knew, all of them, he was sure of it.

Olivia had refused him, and as king, she should have given him whatever he wanted. Even before she'd been mated to his brother, he'd never been able to convince her that he was doing her a great favor by fucking her. She'd never seen it that way, no matter how much he'd tried to force his way upon her. Her arguments had been tiresome to him. First it had been because she was saving herself for her one true love. Then it was that she belonged to another, his brother, and she would not submit to Dakamon. Finally, when she'd moved to the castle with Viktor to be with them all, he'd had enough and he confronted her behind locked doors.

"But I am king." She nodded but didn't bow before him as he had ordered her to. "I command all, and you, Olivia, are part of what I command. Strip off your clothing and get into my bed. I grow weary of waiting for you."

"I cannot, Dakamon, and you are wrong to say such things to me. Your father would have you in shackles if he knew of your latest threats to—" He cut her off with a wave of his hand, but it did little to make her stop pointing out what he so didn't want to hear. "I'm not going to have you. I don't want you, but it's more than that. I'm your sister-in-law and not one of the people who are here to feed you and see to you."

"But I don't want them right now. I want you. And so you know, I do not threaten, my dear sister, I make promises. If you do not get into my bed now, I will have to force you to, and we both know that if need be, I'll bring in the guard to hold you to my bed whilst I have my way." He took a step toward her when she spoke.

"You mean like you had my sister do? How did that work for you, Dakamon? She is a good person, unlike you, and wouldn't do your bidding either." Olivia crossed her arms over her chest and glared. "You're going to have to live with disappointment. I shall not give you what you want. Ever."

She had backed from him, her head held high and her eyes blazing with anger. Taking a step toward her, he realized that now he had to have her for no other reason than she'd refused him. She backed to the wall, and he slapped her when she screamed.

"You'll do as I say now." She didn't cower from him as he wanted her to, but defied him even then. Blood poured from the wound at her head, and he knew that as soon as he took her she'd drink from him and be healed. It was the least he could do for her. But she slapped him back, and a fury like he'd never had before or since seemed to take his body from him.

When he woke from his anger, a kind of coming back unto himself, he found Olivia in the middle of his bed, bloodied and hurt badly. He had hurt her, and it looked as if he'd not only raped her repeatedly but had bitten her all over her lovely body. He realized no amount of his blood would keep her from telling on him, so he tried to think what to do. Other than killing her, like he knew that he should, Dakamon thought about putting her in a cell and forgetting about her. It was all he could do and not be killed himself.

"What have you done?" he asked her. Of course there was no answer from her; she was out cold. "Had you only done what you were told, only did what I wanted, then you'd be free now."

Dakamon had gotten up to pace and noticed all the blood that covered his body. He wondered if she'd hurt him in her need to leave his bed, but after examining himself thoroughly, he found nothing. He still was pissed at her for not just giving him what he wanted, and also for her not being awake long enough for him to question her on her enjoyment of him fucking her.

He couldn't call his servants in to clean up the mess. They would have to report him, and he had no desire to die because his own kin would not heed to his needs. Wrapping her into his sheets, he carried her to the nearest wall and almost dropped her over it to be dealt with by the ones who roamed the grounds, but he found that there were too many people there who would witness what he was about to do. Instead, he took her to the sublevels of his castle and threw her in the smallest darkest cell he could find. He was terrified that Harley would find her before she died, and he had no doubt that she would, sooner rather than later.

She'd known from the start what he'd done. Dakamon knew that as a guardian she would have the powers to track her sister's whereabouts and that worried him greatly. She'd watched him for days and he'd wanted to go to the body and make sure it was just where he'd left it. But he'd seen Harley in the sub levels and had accused her of killing her sister. Before there was a trial, he'd sentenced her and had her banished to this world, and would have stripped her of her magic had his father not interfered.

"You cannot leave her defenseless, son. She's only just lost her sister and...I'm sure that whatever happened, Harley is now regretting it. There are things in that world that we know nothing about." His father was heartbroken over the death of his only daughter-in-law as Dakamon had told him that Harley had confessed what she'd done, and Achard turned to Peter for guidance. "What say you? Send her there without magic or behead her now?"

"She does not deserve to have her death so quick," Peter had said, and Dakamon wanted to smile. The man was helping him without knowing it. "Send her there, but there are to be stipulations."

Dakamon watched his father and Peter come to terms about Harley's sentence, but all Dakamon was concerned about was that she'd be gone soon. When he glanced at her, she was staring at him so hard he was afraid of her. She stood up when the time came for her to be banished and looked at him.

"You'll pay for this. My sister's death, if she is indeed dead, will be avenged. Mark my words, Dakamon Ravengric." She spit in his face just as she disappeared, and there was nothing he could have done to make her pay for that either. And now he feared it was much too late.

Now she was hunting him. He knew what hunting from a guardian meant. She would find him, behead him, then stake his head on a pike outside his home for all to see his shame. Then when he was there until the flesh rotted from his skull, she'd take him to the pits, a large, tar-filled hole, and drop him into it. There would be shame because his name would be added to the roster of those that had been sentenced there before him, and those after him would be added above his name as his was the house of royalty and all would be able to see where he lay. There would be no marker for his passing in the family plot, his body would not reside by that of his ancestors, and no one would mourn his death. Dakamon would be lost from the world.

Here he had no idea what she'd do to him, whether or not he'd be taken back or die here. He had to do something, and do it soon. Begging to his father was his only recourse. Making amends with him would stop whatever madness Harley had in store for him.

Chapter 10

"Will he run?" Harley looked up to see Peter standing near the chair she'd been sitting in while talking to Dakamon. "Do you believe he will go to another realm now that he knows you seek him? He has to know that staying here will be his certain death."

"There is nowhere for him to go. All other worlds will know that he is hunted and will not offer him shelter. I've made sure of that before speaking to him. Anyone who offers him passage or takes him in will meet with Achard, Dakamon's father, and the king will not think favorably of anyone who goes against what he's decreed. It's the way of Ravengric." He nodded and sat down across from her. When she made to stand, he asked her to wait.

"I should like a word with you." He waited for her to sit or go, both options holding both dread and fear for her. "I wish to speak to you about the day you left."

"I did not leave, I was banished. By your command." He nodded and dropped his head. "What could you say to me that would make a difference to me now, Peter? I have been here for nearly fifteen hundred human years without help, without companionship. I have been in exile more than half my life. What could you say to me that would have me sit with you?"

"I would wish that you forgive me." The words were softly spoken, but she could hear the tremor in his voice. "I would ask that you know that I loved your sister with all my heart. And when I came here, it was to find you and to tell you how wrong I was. I...I know that it makes little difference to you now, but I have lived much the same life as you, and if not for the friendship of Rayne Golden, I would have left this world and all others."

"You are right. It makes no difference to me." But it did and she thought he knew it. "I don't need to forgive you, and you asking me is cruel. I lost my sister that day. Nay, I lost everything that day, and you helped take it from me."

"I did not know then what I do now. Dakamon has been...he fooled everyone save you. Not even his own brother knew of the monster that he was. Olivia did as well but we learned too late to save her. Now.... It is within my power to save you and the Goldens." She stared at him, not understanding. "Dakamon will come to his power soon. He'll only need to drink from a fairy to have them back. He does not know this, of course, but the way he is going, it will be too short a time before he falls upon one and drinks her blood. When he does, there will be no one to stop him but you and the Goldens."

"You'd sacrifice them to have a mad man taken into justice?" He was shaking his head even before she finished. "Then what? You expect him to.... Good Christ, you want him to come here, and you think that they'll be able to thwart him?"

"As a family you will. We have protected them for you. The other women of this family, the mates, have been chosen to complement you in this. You and the others will be able to come together to save this world as well as Ravengric." She shook her head at him, but he continued. "Harley, you have to know that what I'm telling you is the truth. You can feel the power when you are all together. It is why you hide in here instead of being with them."

Keith came into the room just then and looked at her and then at Peter. "What's going on here? Harley, what is he doing to you now?"

She didn't answer but waited for Peter to tell him. "We had to do this in order for the worlds to be able to live. Without Harley here you would have died that day. Without all the others, there would be no Golden Streak. There would be nothing left of you. The women of this family are your foundation."

Keith looked at her, then at him. Peter had to feel his anger. She could, and Keith was making no effort to hide it. When he spoke, there was so much venom in his voice she felt her body respond to him in defense, a need to fight with him.

"So you fucked with our lives for some greater good? You think that justifies what you've done to all of us? To Harley? Christ, please tell me you didn't kill Viktor's mate just so the events you had in place were just the—"

"No, my lord. The events of now are the result of Lady Olivia's death. We had no idea what sort of person he was until...Dakamon hid well what he was. It wasn't until after Harley was gone that we realized what lengths he'd gone to to ensure that he was king." Peter dropped to his knees before Keith. "I pledge to you my heart and my trees that I have done nothing to Lady Harley other than to make sure you were to meet her. Nothing else, not the accident nor the death of my beloved Lady Olivia, did I have anything to do with. This I swear."

Keith looked at her over Peter's bent head. *Do you believe him? Do you think he's been moving us around like this for all this time to make sure of…hell, I don't know, make sure that what he wants is given to him?*

I don't think he harmed my sister, but the rest…. She looked at Bronwyn when she and the others entered the room and felt the surge of power move over her. *I know he's right about us all being shit-kicking strong when we're together. Are we that way because he made it so, or that we simply are…I don't know. I guess time will tell.*

Rayne sat down first and looked at the three of them. Harley was still standing, so she moved to where Keith was standing and reached for his hand. Whatever happened in the next few moments would be very telling, she thought. When Bronwyn laughed, they all turned to her.

"You'd think we were going to kill someone. Is that what we're doing?" There was a small surge of power above what they were already creating. Bronwyn lifted a brow at her. "Is that you?"

Harley shook her head. "I think it's all of us. Peter was just telling me that we were all put together to complement each other. To be a force, I suppose, to fight against Dakamon. Keith and I were trying to figure out just how far he went to make this happen." Rayne looked at Peter with narrow eyes. She had been his friend the longest, yet she seemed to be surprised by this as much as the rest of them. "I don't think he hurt Keith if that's what you're thinking, but the rest…I simply don't know."

"Can you read his mind?" Harley shook her head at Ally's question. "You can't or you won't?"

"Can't. He's part of the royal court, and it's forbidden for me to do it. It's certain death if I try. Same goes for Ryland and Bronwyn. They're considered something of royal beings, and I'm not…equipped I guess you could say, to look."

"But I can." Rayne stood up to move, Harley supposed to Peter, but was stopped by the appearance of Viktor and the king. Neither man looked all that happy. "He knows something and we're going to find out what it is. Either move back or we test this theory on how fucking strong we are together."

Harley felt the moment that Lenny stood up along with Em. The women were no longer holding back but letting a little of themselves go. When both Ally and Bronwyn did the same, they pulled her into their strength so that she was humming with it too. Yet she knew for some reason she was the one controlling them. When Rayne turned to wink at her, she took a step toward the king.

"Let her search or I don't know if I can hold this. I've never felt…Christ, they're pulling me apart." When Keith touched her arms, she felt the power or whatever it was take him as well. And because of his connection to his brothers, they joined her in the surge. "Fuck, help me."

The room grew dark, then brightened so much that she closed her eyes against it. There were people talking, some of them loudly, but all she could do was try to hold on. Looking at the king, she knew he was happy with this, and she touched him. The scream in her head took her to the floor.

~~~

Achard watched her rest. He'd never been so terrified in all his life than when she touched him. And thrilled. Christ, she could more than likely light the entire world with the power she'd had when her fingers brushed against his bare skin. Her young cat sat next to her as she lay on the bed and glared at him when he turned to look. But he'd not said a word.

"I can explain if you'd allow it." Keith shook his head. "I would like to tell you what we did."

"I don't care. Whatever it is, you're very lucky that I was able to stop them from killing you down there. And as of right now, I'm thinking you can deal with your son on your own. I don't really give a good fuck what happens to you or your world." Keith stretched his neck, and Achard heard it pop. "I'm so close to killing you myself right now that I can hardly hold back my cat."

"I'll kill him and you if you attack me." It was softly spoken, but Keith heard him. "You and she are not your normal pair, none of you are. We only did it to enhance you so that your line would live forever. But things progressed in a different direction once Viktor and Peter figured out what had really happened." Keith glanced at him but said nothing as he continued. "I wasn't aware of what they had set up here other than to make it so the Golden family was protected. Only later, after I'd found out how Olivia had died, was I made aware of what was going on. Viktor had planned to bring Dakamon down, but I had...it was because of me and him coming to this world that made it so that he is going to have to stand trial here and not in Ravengric. I'm sorry for that."

"Is she going to be all right? I know that you said she was when this happened, but how do I know that this is not another one of your lies to get what you want?" Achard was hurt by the man not believing him, but was not surprised by his words. "She was bleeding from her ears and nose. Christ, even her eyes were bleeding. That does not sound like she was fine."

"She came into her power is all. A great deal of it, as a matter of fact. The others got it as well, but she…she shielded you all from the pain of it." Keith turned to look at him and Achard could see his question forming, but answered it before he could ask. "She gave you as much as she received, but kept you all from hurting with it. She took it all into herself."

"Keith?" They both stood up when Harley spoke. "Are you okay? Did I hurt you or any of the others?"

"No, love, we're all just fine." Achard moved to the door to leave when he heard his name. He turned back to the couple when Harley spoke.

"Dakamon is going to die. You know that, don't you? As soon as I find him…*we* find him…we're going to kill him. Are you going to take me back with you to stand trial if I do?"

"No." She nodded at him, more than likely knowing there was more to it than his answer. "I'll see you both later."

After he walked out of the room and shut the door behind him, Achard looked at Ryland, who stood there as if waiting. The man was pissed, that much was obvious. But whether it was at him or at all of them was the question. When the male started down the hall, Achard followed, figuring he'd be lucky if he ever made it back to Ravengric in one piece. As soon as he entered the large office, he could see he was almost right. He wasn't going to make it back in one piece, and he might not at all. The Goldens were assembled around the room like a firing squad.

"I can explain. I can—" Ryland cut him off and moved to the desk and sat. Achard did as well, and the rest of them moved the chairs that had been brought from the dining room to this room. That's when he noticed Peter. The man was as distraught as he'd ever seen him.

"I had no idea that she'd be that powerful. I thought she'd gain strength from the rest of them, but…did you know that the others would feed her as well?" Achard sat down and stared at him. He'd no idea that any of this was possible before it happened, but apparently Peter did. And when Viktor came into the room, he had an idea that he knew as well. But before he could answer, Sandra stood up.

"You two are no longer welcome here after this is over." Viktor stood up, but she wasn't finished yet. "I've had my family hurt, nearly killed, and there is a young woman up there that had been hurt by you two long before you came here to mess with our lives. I'm finished with you all." She looked at Achard. "And you? How could you allow this to happen? That boy of yours should have been discovered long before now, and you sat back on your bottom and let him…I'm so angry right now that I could slap you all and not care what you did to me for it."

"He didn't know what was—"

Sandra cut Viktor off. "He most certainly did. Every parent knows when their child is doing things he or she isn't supposed to. That son of yours killed your other sons, and yet here you sit waiting for someone else to take him to the wood shed." The room seemed to brighten considerably for several seconds, and Achard's mate appeared in front of Sandra.

"You're absolutely right, my dear. I've told him several times that it was a mistake to make Dakamon king, but he said it was his rite of passage." His mate looked at him and he knew real fear. "I told you this would happen, and now look what's going on."

Achard stood up. He kissed Parthinia on the cheek and then her hand. His mate was something to behold when she was upset, as she appeared to be now. He introduced her to the family present, as well as Keith when he and Harley came in. Harley bowed before her and didn't rise until Parthinia bid her to.

"You've grown more beautiful since I saw you last." Harley blushed and started to move away. "Nay, child, I would like a hug from you. I have missed you so much."

The women embraced, and the power surged again but not nearly so strongly. Achard looked around the room and knew that the others had felt it as well. When his mate bid them to sit, he found the room a little more relaxed than before.

"I've come here for several reasons. There is a warrant out for Dakamon's immediate death if he should go to other worlds to seek sanctuary." She looked at Harley and then at him. "I suppose you know about this?"

"I do. I told her to do it." Harley stood, but before he could tell her he was handling it, she spoke.

"Beg your forgiveness, my lady, but he didn't know until after I'd set the warrant into motion. I had already made the arrangements with the other off-worlds before I spoke to the king. I was fearful of Dakamon going to other realms and causing untold amounts of problems with Ravengric." She glanced at him as she continued. "Dakamon has already contacted four of the other realms and has been turned away. He will be here until we can capture him."

"Do you have an idea where he is?" Harley didn't answer her but looked at Keith. "You are the computer whiz, are you not?"

"I am, I suppose, but everyone here calls me a geek or a nerd. I can answer to either. But mostly I'm her mate. And will protect her to the best of my ability." He looked around the room, glaring at Achard before looking at Parthinia to continue. "We all will work together to protect each other despite the recent interference."

"And there has been a great deal of that." Parthinia sat down and smiled at Sandra. She and the woman seemed to come to some kind of agreement before Parthinia spoke again, looking around the room. "Dakamon will not stand trial. I would very much appreciate it if he was dealt with immediately upon his capture. There has been too much grief, as well as it has been going on much too long now. Are you prepared to do what must be done?"

"So you wish your own son dead." It wasn't a question from Sandra, but before Parthinia or even anyone else could answer, she continued. "I don't know if I could be that cold. Other than the deaths of the humans here and poor Viktor's mate, what has he done?"

"Murder is the least of his crimes, but no less serious. He has murdered three of his brothers, each murder more heinous than the one before. The first one, Mylo, he murdered simply by slicing his head from his body. It was made to look like he'd been robbed and killed. His brother Angelo was killed with his entire family. Three of my grandchildren along with them. He locked them into a cell without light or air, and when they were found years later, we figured out that my son and his wife had killed their children to keep them from suffering. And suffering they would have done, too. His wife was next, and then he simply let himself die, but not by his own hand, which would have been considerably quicker than by letting himself starve to death." Achard handed her a handkerchief as she started to cry. "Then our baby still living at home with us. He…he murdered him…."

"He hung him by his feet and cut him at his throat in a way that caused him to die slowly, bleeding to death over a five-day period. We didn't know, of course, that he'd done it, but Dakamon was the one who found each of them. Who would think that a child could do such things to his own…his brothers? How could he?" Achard held his wife until both their tears subsided. He looked up at Sandra when she moved to sit beside him on the floor.

"I'm so very sorry for your loss. It must have been hard…no, I don't know what you felt when you found out. I don't think there are words that could convey how very sorry I am." Sandra nodded at him and then stood up and faced her family. "I think we should roast the fucker."

Harley stood up and stretched her arms above her head, and he felt the magic rain down on the entire room. When she faced him, she bowed low before turning to the room and her mate. This was what Peter and Viktor had hoped would happen, he just knew it.

"When he comes here he won't know what we share. I've made sure of that." Ryland stood up, and she cocked a brow at him. "You think to tell me to stay home so that you men can take care of this, I will put you into a world of hurt, tiger."

He kissed her nose, to the shock of all those present. "Nah, I was thinking we could all sit here and wait until you rid us of this shit, and then we'd have drinks on the deck afterwards. Smart ass. I think we should eat, then plan; or plan while we eat. I don't know about the rest of you, but I'm hungry. Also…." Ryland looked at Keith, then at Harley again. "I have to discuss something with you. And I'd like to do that before the shit hits the fan."

"I think that's an excellent idea." Sandra ushered the others out of the room, save Achard and his mate and Bronwyn. She sat back on the sofa as if she were king of the world. Achard supposed in a way, in her own world, she was pretty much that. When the door closed behind the others, Ryland spoke.

"He's going to come here on our turf. When he does, I'd like to be as prepared for him as we can be." They all nodded their agreement. "That being said, what the fuck did you give us all when you touched us with that powerbase? I'm assuming that you know."

"Yes," Harley answered Ryland with a smile. "But you're not going to like it."

Ryland snorted and Bronwyn laughed as she answered for Ryland. "He's a great man, but he doesn't like a lot of things. Not knowing is making his cat pissy. And when he's pissy, I'm pissy."

"I don't know what you not being pissy looks like now that you mention it." This time Achard and Parthinia laughed as Harley continued. "We're all the same. Each of you will have what you were before but a great deal more. All of us are immortals, as well as shifters. You have fangs if you need them, and you can move through space much like I do."

"Much like you have? Meaning, you have more of us?" Harley nodded, then glanced at Achard and his mate. "They have something to do with this?"

"She gave me more when she hugged me. I want to think it was a mistake, but I doubt she'd make a mistake like that one. I have everything you are times ten." Achard could see that all of them were trying to work it out in their head just how powerful Harley was when she put out her hand. "Touch me."

Chapter 11

Dakamon was stalking the woman who had been eluding him for two days now. He wasn't sure what it was about her that he wanted more than the others, but she was something. He had finally gotten her trapped in a bar last night, only to have her disappear almost as soon as they entered. Dakamon had had to leave the place as the crush of humans had made him ill. Tonight he was better prepared for it, but she'd moved into an open market that was just closing down. As soon as he was close enough to smell her, she turned to look where he was standing. The look in her eyes made him want to cower away from her.

When she moved again, there was a quickness about her, but she wasn't going to get away from him this time, and he moved with her. He moved in behind her as she turned into a busy coffee shop he'd seen earlier. As soon as he touched her, his fangs dropped.

"Come with me or I take you and everyone else in this room with you. I'd certainly hate to see all these humans killed because you let it happen." Actually Dakamon didn't care about the humans at all, but she nodded once and went with him. As soon as he had her out of the building, he dragged her around the corner to the alley and pressed her against the wall.

"Don't do this. You've no idea what biting me will do to you." She begged so much like Olivia that he nearly let her go. "I can pay you. I have money."

"I don't want your fucking money. I want to drain you." She shook her head and he smiled. "You think that I won't? I got news for you. This is going to be the best meal of my life, as well as a hell of a fuck."

He tried to snare her into his eyes, but she was too strong. But he did tear at her clothes enough to get her pants off. He didn't care so long as somewhere he could put his dick was open, because he was harder than he'd ever been in his life. And when he put his nose to her throat to bite her, she nearly made him come with only her scent.

"Fuck, you smell delicious." She tried to push him away, but he was stronger than she was. "I'm going to enjoy this."

As soon as he licked her throat, his cock exploded. His climax was so powerful that he nearly blacked out from it, and he'd never even stuck it in her. Biting her now was all he could think about, and he sank his fangs deep into her throat and came again.

Christ, he thought as he held her to him and emptied himself over her. Taking a deep draw at her throat, he felt dizzy with it. As soon as he swallowed all of his power rocked into him, and he threw back his head and screamed.

He couldn't move, not to chase after her or even to stand upright. Every part of his body hurt and felt rejuvenated at the same time. Every breath he took seemed to tear at his lungs, and even his hair hurt him in some vague way. Dropping to his knees, he held onto the wall, but he was weaker now as the pain stopped and he fell to the dirty ground, his head hitting hard.

Dakamon lay there. He was sure that whatever had happened was over, but he was afraid to take the chance. While he did feel much like his old self, he was still not completely restored. He lay there for several more minutes, just letting his body adjust to the magic before he finally stood up.

No longer dizzy but still weak, he moved along the wall to stand in the street. He had no idea how long he'd been there, but he thought it couldn't have been much more than a few minutes. But looking at the darkened streets with their lights on, he knew it had been much longer. He'd taken the girl in the alley around dusk, but now he thought it close to sunrise.

Walking with a slight stagger, he made his way back to the home he'd been staying in. He thought about the girl once but no more. By now she'd be dead, as he didn't remember sealing the wounds.

"Serves her right for running. And then not letting me fuck her." He was actually a little relieved by thinking that had he entered her, he might not have survived it. Just licking her had nearly killed him; fucking her would have most likely killed him for sure. He was nearly to his home when he realized something. He was restored. Not fully—and he blamed her for that as well—but he felt better than he had since arriving here.

By the time he got to the house he was stronger. He didn't feel the need to feed again even though he'd only had a sip of her blood. Going to the sublevels to rest, he felt his father nearby, as well as Harley. First thing he was going to do when he rose this evening was find them both. There was someone else there, but he couldn't tell who they were, only that they were stronger than him.

"I'll be strong enough to take them on as soon as I rest." He felt better for saying it aloud, but had no idea how true it was. "Just wait now, you fucking cunt. When I find you you'll be as dead to me as that sister of yours."

Closing his eyes, he tried to figure out who the new power was, but it was too exhausting and he really didn't care. All he wanted now was to take care of Harley and then his brother. If his father didn't change his mind about him being king, then he too would be killed. Dakamon was the true and only king, and if they had a problem with that, so be it.

Sometime during his rest he felt the power again and knew it was closer to him, but he was too drained to let it bother him overly much, as no one came to him. He had a thought that he was nearly out in the open and vulnerable, but he closed his eyes again and rested. By the time the sun was lowering again, he woke suddenly to feel he was no longer alone in the house.

"Who's there?" A soft laugh had him curling into himself, only to realize that whoever was there wasn't going to harm him or they would have already. Before he could command they come to him, he heard him laugh again.

"You think that you're safe from us?" He didn't know the voice or the man when he stepped into the dim light. "I think I'm going to enjoy taking you down."

"You think so, do you? I'll have you know that I'm king of my own realm and you'll do well to remember that. What are you doing here?" Dakamon stood up and the man laughed again. He only just then realized he was naked. "What do you want?"

"Why, you dead, to start with." The man took another step toward him, and that's when Dakamon realized the man wasn't really there; it was only a projection of him. "But I'm not less powerful in this state."

He'd read his mind. The man, the being, had read his mind, and Dakamon wondered what else he could do. When he sat down, Dakamon moved to the edge of his bed and looked at him. He still didn't know who he was, but decided to forgo telling him anything to see what he might know first.

"I'm not as forthcoming as you'd think. There are others helping me have a conversation with you, and you'd be surprised at how much they want you dead as well." Dakamon searched the room he was in and saw no one else. When he stood up, the man sat, and that irritated him to no end.

"I did not give you leave to sit down while I'm standing. Get up." The man continued to sit. "Did you hear me? I said to get on your feet until I say you can sit in my presence."

"I guess you think you're still in charge. No problem I guess, for now. And I don't want to stand so I'll just remain here." When he laughed again, Dakamon moved forward to slap him, only to move through his body. "You might want to save your energy for later. I'm thinking you're going to need it when we come after you."

"You? You think to beat me? I've regained what was taken from me. You've no power over me." The man nodded. "Who are you, anyway, that you think to speak to me in such a way?"

"Keith Golden. And in the event that doesn't ring a bell, perhaps knowing that I'm Harley Pennington's mate and soon-to-be husband is what will tell you. You do know her, don't you?"

"She was forbidden to take a mate. When I'm restored to Ravengric, I'll make sure you're both punished to the fullest, and we'll see how much she thinks she can get by with then." Dakamon felt his energy hum around him and wished that the man was there. "Why do you not just come here instead of hovering about like a spectrum?"

"And ruin the fun for the others? I don't think so. We've a welcoming party for you if you dare to come to us. You should see all the people that have come to watch us kill you. It's like we're having a huge party and you're the guest of honor." Keith laughed again. "Of course, you're not a welcome guest, but one we'll give what you so richly deserve for sure."

Dakamon would be a fool to go, and he was pretty sure he'd be dead before he entered whatever domain the man had. He was nearly ready to tell him he'd bring them here to talk, but the man shook his head.

"Harley said you're too chicken-shit to come. Oh, in case you don't understand, she said you were a big terrified baby and wouldn't step foot on our property. I told her you probably are, but that you'd have to come for sure when you found out we were having cake, too. You like cake, don't you?"

He had no idea what "cake" was, but he was sure he didn't want any part of it. But he also didn't want her to assume he was too afraid to come. He'd just come on his terms, not hers. Smiling, he looked at Keith.

"Oh, I would love to come. And I'll have a drink of cake with her too if she wants." He smiled when the man laughed. "I'll have to finish up a few things here, but I'll be there soon. Say tomorrow night? Will that be all right?"

Keith stood up and Dakamon had a flash of fear. The man was huge, and he could now feel that he was cat...tiger. When the man put out his hand, Dakamon nearly reached for it, but at the last second pulled his hand back.

"You're going to insult me? Or are you afraid of me?" The challenge was there but Dakamon wasn't going to go for it. "I guess your father was right too."

"My father? You've spoken to...." Then he remembered that his father was there with Viktor. "My father said I wouldn't take the hand of a man who is no more here than he is? I think you're off your mind if you think I'm going to be made a fool by reaching for a hand that is not there."

Keith's hand took his, and Dakamon felt the power from the man rush over him. The man wasn't just a cat but so much more. As he staggered back, Dakamon stumbled over his own shoes and fell to the floor. Keith's laughter could be heard throughout the room as he faded away.

"I'm going to kill that man if it's the last thing I do." He was very afraid that it might just be.

~~~

"He was still sleeping when I woke him." Keith smiled at Harley when she told him again that Dakamon was dangerous and was resting, not sleeping. "He sleeps in the nude, too."

She dropped the brush she was using and turned to him. She had the most shocked look on her face that he nearly laughed at her, but didn't. She didn't look to be in the best of humor. Again.

"You saw his body?" He nodded, not knowing why she suddenly sounded so excited. "Did he have a mark here?"

She put her hand over her breast, then made a slashing mark to her belly. He tried to think and remembered something being there, and closed his eyes trying to think if it was the light or the man.

"Yeah, it's about two inches wide and about two feet long. He's really overweight too, so the thing is all stretched out and saggy." She clapped her hands and he looked at her. "I take it you gave that to him."

"I did. He'd been trying to get me to bring Olivia to him before and I'd refused. He'd taken out his sword that he wore around his waist and slapped me with it. I couldn't fight back, of course, but I did manage to fall against him and the blade cut into him deeply. I was punished by the other guards for harming him, but not too badly." She smiled at him in the mirror in front of her. "They thought it grand that I had gotten first blood from him."

Keith walked up behind her and put his hands on her shoulders as she set the brush down on the table in front of her. She watched him as he smoothed his hand down her shoulders to her breasts and cupped them.

"You should know that I'm going to enjoy watching you take the bastard down." She nodded and leaned back into his groin. "Harley, I want you. Would you like me here or in the woods as a cat?"

"Both." He pinched her nipples and she moaned. "Keith, please don't tease me right now. I'm so on edge that I can't think."

He knew she was. And not because of sex, but because she was afraid for them all. He was as well, but not as badly as she seemed to be. He put his fingers in the top of his pajama top she had on and tore it open. Her breasts spilled out into his waiting hands.

"I can think of all kinds of ways to relieve your tension. Would you like for me to help you?" She nodded and rolled her hips over his cock more firmly. "Stand up, baby. I want to watch you while I take you this way."

Keith took a step back and watched her stand. Her breasts moved with each movement, and he felt his mouth water to taste her. When she leaned over the vanity he had moved in here for her, he could see her nipples had hardened to tight peaks and they'd turned a dark red. Curling his fingers into her panties, he tore them from her as well, then pulled the shirt off.

"Christ, do you have any idea how lovely you look right now? How badly I want to ram my cock into you and stay there?" She moaned and he felt it all the way to his toes. "Spread your legs for me. I want to play first."

"Please, just take me. I'm so wet I can feel it on my thighs." He could smell her too, her arousal so hot and strong that he had to free his cock or risk hurting himself. "Keith, let me take you into my mouth, please?"

He didn't answer her because in truth he wanted to beg her to do just that. When he dropped to his knees and licked the cream running down her thigh, he heard her beg him to finish her. Sliding his fingers up over her and into her sheath, he licked her rear cheek and nipped hard.

"I'm going to drink from you first. Then I'm going to fuck you hard enough that you come so much you're going to beg me to stop." He doubted he would make it that long, but he was going to try. "Then once you come enough I'm going to mark you again. Sink my teeth into your flesh and mark you for everyone to see that you belong to me."

"I do. I want to belong to you." She was panting and he felt his cat snarl at him to get with it. "Please Keith, you're teasing me."

Rocking his fingers in and out of her, he spread her legs wider only to realize he just couldn't reach his goal. Turning her around, he had her sit on the top of the vanity and put her feet on his shoulders. If there was anything more beautiful, he wasn't sure he wanted to see it.

She was spread for him; her curls, wet with her cream, glistened in the candlelight from the candles he'd lit before touching her. Her clit was hard and sticking above her nether lips, begging to be suckled, and he didn't want to disappoint. Leaning in slowly, he licked the tiny nubbin and looked up at her when she cried out.

"Come for me. I want to drink all I can, so come for me." Taking her clit into his mouth again, he sucked hard. As soon as her thighs tightened around his head, he felt her fingers curl into his hair. When she came, he heard her scream out his name and drank greedily from her.

Over and over he commanded her to come, and each time her body responded as if he'd flipped a switch. When she begged him to stop, pleaded with him that she couldn't take any more, he stood up and pulled her off the seat and onto his cock. The three steps to the wall had him nearly tripping over his pants until he managed to get himself free. As soon as her back touched the wall, he took her mouth.

"Come for me again. I want to feel you tighten around my cock." She moaned and her body bowed up and she screamed. Keith felt his own climax race to release. And when he licked her throat his fangs dropped. His cat snarled at her as she tore back his head and licked his throat. As soon as she sank her teeth into him he came. His balls, already tight to his body, seemed to curl up into him in an effort to fill her. When she offered him her wrist, he bit her, coming again, his body pressing hers so tightly against the wall he wondered if it would support them.

As soon as she sealed the wound at his throat, he licked the one at her wrist closed and held her to him for several seconds. His heart was pounding so hard that he doubted he could do much more than this. Walking even the short distance to the bed seemed to be an effort. When she kissed his shoulder and lifted her head, he looked at her and fell into love with her all over.

"You certainly know how to relax a girl." Keith grinned at her. "I love you, Keith. I never thought I'd be lucky enough to have a man like you in my life, but to be in love with you too is almost unbelievable."

"Marry me." She grinned at him. "I love you as much as you do me, so let's get married. Today. Now, if we can manage it."

They both looked at the door when the clock down the hall chimed out the hour. It told them that at two in the morning they'd have to wait until at least the sun came up. Taking her to the bed and never letting her go, he lay down with her and held her. She was asleep long before he could get his own mind to slow down.

He was thinking about how to get a license when he felt her stiffen. Then he felt it too. A strong surge of power seemed to settle over him and he felt...well, dirty, he supposed, would be as good as name as any. When she sat up and looked around the room, he did as well, tense for several seconds until he realized what they were feeling.

"Dakamon has drunk from a faerie." Harley nodded. "Did he kill her? Can we find her if he didn't?"

"She'll know to come here. I put out the word yesterday to all the realms that if one of theirs was bitten they were to send them to us. Dead or alive." Harley turned to him. "It's begun. He'll be strong now and seeking revenge. Are you sure you want to stand with me?"

Keith kissed her rather than answer her. He reached for his brother to let him know what had happened. *We felt it too. We didn't know what, but...is Harley okay? I bet she's upset.*

She's.... Keith laughed. *She's energized, I think. I'm thinking that when he does get here, he's not going to know what the fuck he's up against.*

I bet she wants this finished as much as we do. Keith told him he did as well and then told him about the faerie. *I'll make sure that the guards around the grounds know to look out for her. I hope to Christ he didn't kill her.*

Keith hoped so as well and closed the connection between him and his brother. Harley was pacing the room, and he watched her naked body move to and fro. When she stopped suddenly and smiled at him, he was a little afraid.

"She's here. The faerie." She moved to his closet. "Have you ever met one? A faerie, I mean, have you ever met one?"

"No, I don't think so." She told him he'd know if he had. "Why do I get the feeling that this isn't going to be like meeting Viktor or the king?"

"Trust me, it's nothing like meeting one of them. Especially who this girl is. You're in for a treat. This girl is royalty, and she's fucking pissed off."

The door was being pounded on as they went down the stairs. When Keith opened the door, a woman sped past him and flew at Harley. The two of them tumbled to the floor and he nearly went to Harley's aid when he realized they were laughing. Christ, this was going to be a long night.

Chapter 12

"I'm telling you right now, he's a fat log." Bronwyn watched the faerie, Maven, shove more food into her mouth as she continued. "I saw him the night before but never thought a thing about it until I saw him tonight too. Did you know that he thinks he's doing us a favor by drinking from us?"

"Did he know what you were?" Maven shook her head at her. "Then I don't understand how he found you to drink from you."

"Faeries have this sort of scent about them. It calls to vampires, even though they usually can't drink from them...not without permission. When Dakamon drank from Maven without permission, he did get his powers back, but because I'd warned all the kings of the realms that he might take one of their own, it was agreed upon that they would be...tainted." Harley looked at Maven, then back at Bronwyn before she continued. "She's poisoned him, but he won't know it right away."

"You tricked him." Harley nodded and Bronwyn burst out laughing. "I knew there was a reason I liked you. Nice trick. So what happens to him? He slowly dies until he's no longer a threat to us?"

"No, not quite." Harley got up to pace the room, and Bronwyn had a feeling that she wasn't going to like this. "He has to...he's going to just be really sick. For a long time. I can't just kill him, no matter how much I want to. If I did that, it would be unfair. And fairness is what Ravengric is about. To everyone, even the criminals."

"So, he's going to be sick. Just sick?" Harley nodded. "And this is helpful to us how? I mean, I've seen some sick people before, so at least tell me it's really bad."

"It won't be enough to kill him, no. But he'll be ill for a time. And he won't be able to heal from a bite either. Not right away anyway." Harley looked at her as she continued. "I know that this isn't want you need to hear, but I swear to you, it's the best that I can do."

"So he's not going to be dead but he will be sick. And biting will.... You know, this would go a great deal faster if you simply told me what the fuck is going to happen."

"He will live to come back here and try this all again." Peter glared at Harley before he looked at Maven. His sudden appearance in the room had Maven standing up. "What are you doing here? I thought you were told to stay away from me."

"By order of my king I was to come here when I was bitten by a vamp. Not even you can override him, you overbearing, crossed-eyed, blood-sucking asshole." Bronwyn was impressed as well as hysterical at the girl's vocabulary. "You're to stay over one thousand feet back from me or I get to zap your skinny ass."

"It was ten feet, not one thousand, and you're only to call in your father, not touch me at all." Peter looked at Bronwyn. "Can you do something with her? She's not supposed to be here. I don't want her here either."

"I think she's doing just fine on her own." Peter huffed at her. "I take it you two know each other?"

"She's my mate, but her father forbids us to be together, so I've been staying away. *Like I'm supposed to.*" The last part he yelled loud enough to silence the room and bring the rest of the household running. To know that Peter had a mate was one thing, but that they'd been forbidden to be together was altogether a different colored horse.

The shrill whistle had them all turning to Harley. It was a method she used often enough to make them a bit jealous at how loud she'd done it. When she ordered everyone to sit down, Bronwyn noticed that Peter, for all his anger at the young faerie, made sure she sat before him. Curious and curiouser.

"Now, we're going to be calm and quiet from now on. Peter, you are not going to be welcome here if you do not shut up." Bronwyn nearly burst out laughing when his mouth snapped shut with an audible snap. "Maven, if you don't keep a civil tongue in your mouth I'll shut it for you. Do I make myself clear?"

"He isn't—" A look from Keith and she shut up. About the time Harley started to explain what had happened and what was going to happen, Ryland touched Bronwyn's mind.

Do you suppose that Harley has any idea how powerful she is at the moment? That she's ordered beings around as if they were nothing more than children in a school yard? Bronwyn laughed at his description, because that was what they were all acting like. *Even you have quieted down, and that's not like you.*

I was laughing so hard I nearly wet myself when Maven started calling Peter names. Do you suppose they really are mates? He said he had no idea. *I would think it would explain a great deal if he was. The way he seems to stand off from the rest of us as if he's terribly sad. Why do you think they've been forbidden to see each other?*

He's a vampire and she's a faerie comes to mind. She said her father ordered it. I wonder if, given the right motivation, the two of them would come together despite the rules. She liked to think so and told him. *Perhaps when this is finished we can figure out a way to bring the two of them together.*

It might be something to look forward to. And just so you know, I'm looking forward to this being over as well. I want to sleep at night without fear of someone coming to us and tearing our throats out. She listened to Harley as she explained what had happened.

"He had only a sip, not enough to make him all powerful but enough to give him some of what he was. He'll believe, I hope, that more will come to him over the days, and I've a feeling he'll be looking for more of the same blood, faerie blood."

"He'll not get mine again. I wouldn't even have given him what he took had it not been for the fact that I was under the impression he had to ask before he bit." Maven glared at Peter before looking at Bronwyn and Ryland. "I've a mind to stay here until this is over. Sort of hide out, if you wouldn't mind the company."

It was on the tip of her tongue to tell her no, but Peter hopped up and told her there was no way. "You'll not stay with these fine people unless it's over my dead body."

"That can happen, you jackass." Maven took a step toward Peter and him to her. The two of them were inches apart and shouting at each other at the top of their lungs. When Harley stepped back, Bronwyn was sure she was going to tell them to shut up again, but suddenly they were both gone. Keith sat in the chair that Maven had been in, picked up her last slice of bacon, and began eating it.

"Hum, what happened to them?" Harley grinned at her, and Bronwyn had a sudden thought. "You didn't."

"I did. And they'll either come out as mates or one or both of them will be dead. I told her father that if I saw them together and they seemed to be fighting again, I'd arrange things. He said to have at it. Her father, by the way, is going to come calling when Dakamon is taken care of. He wants to meet the white tigers." Harley took a piece of toast off the counter as she continued. "Agnar, the king of the Southern Faeries, said that he'd heard of you and the streak and wants to become friends. He's not coming now for fear of having his daughter demand that he make Peter stay away again. Agnar wants them together as much as they do. He wants grandchildren."

Ryland cleared his throat as he laughed. There was a great deal more to worry about than two people bent on killing each other, but the distraction was nice. As they talked about where Harley had taken the couple, both Viktor and his parents arrived, along with the Cooks. Lucky for them all, Keith's cook showed up and started cooking breakfast for them.

"Dakamon will be coming here soon. As early as tomorrow night I believe. I've heard that he's on the move, and with the tracker that Harley put on him we've a better idea when he gets here rather than be surprised." Achard sat down, and Bronwyn's heart went out to him as he continued. "They've tallied up the women and men he's killed. Counting the couple and the two children he's murdered at the house he was living in, there are over fifty deaths. Then the ones in my realm add up to over one thousand."

"So many." Em looked around the room, then at Brock as she pulled out a file. "We had the names of the victims here, but not the ones in your realm. We'll need that before we can go to the Realm. For some stupid reason they want them all before they will sentence him."

"There won't be a trial." Everyone looked at Harley when she spoke. "He won't be brought to trial. Once he is found he'll need to be killed on sight. If not, there is the chance that he'll be able to talk them out of his execution and they'll simply put him away. I can't have that, and I'm pretty sure you can't either."

"But he'll be behind bars." Sandra looked at everyone when no one commented on her statement. "He won't be able to get out, will he? He'll be held for all his life."

"They thought they had me behind bars too, as well as Rayne. But we both managed to escape." Sandra was shaking her head as Bronwyn nodded. "You can't think that sometime down the line he won't find someone that will let him out. He'll be able to charm someone into opening the door for him. He'll do it and then what? He'll be more pissed off than he is now, and will kill our family for being the ones that put him there."

"No trial. I don't know...Alistair, what do you think of that? You're a man of the law, what do you think of a man being sentenced to death without so much as a hearing for him to explain what he's being killed for?" Sandra stood up when he didn't answer her. "I see. You all...I'm not sure what to think. A man deserves a trial no matter what his crimes. It's the way of the streak, as well as humans."

When she left the room, Bronwyn looked at Harley, who stared at the door Sandra had left through. She could see her pain and when she looked at her, Bronwyn had a feeling that she was feeling it much deeper than anyone could guess. Before she could tell her that Sandra would come around, she

160

suddenly disappeared. As soon as Keith stood up too, Bronwyn had a feeling that Dakamon was here a great deal sooner than they'd all thought.

~~~

Harley waited for them to settle. Dakamon couldn't bite her, not without her permission, but he could hurt her. As soon as he dropped her, she knew that he was going to hurt her a great deal. The blade entered her left arm as she reached for him.

"Did you honestly think I wouldn't be able to kill you?" His boot connected with her ribs, and she heard two break as he screamed at her. "Did you think after all this time that I'd not be able to track you, find you? You're fucking stupid if you thought that."

This time when he lashed out at her, he knocked her across the room and she hit the wall with a hard punch. Plaster rained down on her head as she fell forward. If he kept this up she'd be dead before she could make him an offer.

He knocked her around the room for another ten minutes, breaking not only ribs but her jaw and her arm as well. Three of her fingers were shattered when he ground them into the floor, and her lip was bleeding so profusely that she was sure she would pass out. He leaned over her when he had beaten her so badly she no longer tried to get away from him.

"You won't fight me, will you? The decree is still in place that forbids you to fight me." He laughed heartily, and she cringed from his putrid breath. "You'll just have to take it until I've had my ton of flesh, and there is nothing at all you can do about it."

"Pound of flesh, you moron." He kicked her in the head and she thought she might live longer if she learned to shut up, but what fun was that? "Your mother said you needed to be drowned at birth. I was afraid it would kill all the poor fishes if you were to enter their domain."

The savage growl was all the warning she got as he charged her. She managed to avoid the blade again, but his fist was another thing. She'd taken hard blows before, but the one he delivered to her head had her seeing stars and hearing a band play taps. Smiling, she closed her eyes, no longer able to hold on. This was really going to piss him off.

The next time she opened her eyes, he was sitting in a large overstuffed chair staring out the window. He looked like the man she had known all those decades ago. Younger in appearance than he was in years by a great deal, but his meanness was gone as well. She must have made a noise because he turned to look at her when she sat up.

"You will bring me my father. Go and get him and return with him posthaste." She shook her head and felt dizziness swamp her. "You heard me, go and get him now."

"I can't and you know why. He took away your title, and even though you are of royal blood, I can't put your safety above his." Harley noticed that she'd been chained to the wall and that he'd hurt her more while she'd been out. Now in addition to the other wounds, her left leg was broken.

"Then I'm asking you to go and get him so that I can talk to him and no more." Nice way to put it, she supposed, but she still wasn't going to go. Not that she could, but he had asked her so nicely.

"I can't, Dakamon. Not because I know you plan to kill him, but you've trashed my body and I won't be able to do it." To make her point, she lifted her arm to have it swing freely below her elbow. "He wouldn't come anyway."

"I want him here." She nearly laughed at his tone. He sounded five years old again, and she wanted to see if he'd stomp his foot too. "My mother then. She's not worth much, just being a woman. Bring her to me so that I can hold her hostage so that Father will come here to save her. If she dies, you can't hurt me for it."

"What are you talking about?" He nodded at her as if that was to explain it. "You think your mother is unworthy of you? You think it's okay to kill her because she's a female?"

"Of course she's unworthy of me. Her purpose has been served in breeding sons to my father. He may come for her, yes, but she's not really any one he'd lose any sleep over if she died." Dakamon snorted at her. "You aren't really worth much either except for the fact that you're a guardian and therefore a little better than most, but not…. You really didn't believe that you'd fetch any sort of price, did you?"

"Price for what?" He looked out the window again. "Price for what, Dakamon? Did you sell me and the other Golden women?"

"I did. Those other women too. It took me a while to figure out the money system, but he was nice enough to show me how it worked and I'm getting top dollar for the six of you. As soon as my father makes the announcement that I'm king, you and those others will be shipped off to somewhere and used for all sorts of experiments. He said that he could make you breed too."

The hair on her arms moved and the ones on her neck stood up. She looked around the room, trying to think who he might have spoken to or better yet, who would have been willing to pay for them. As soon as the name occurred to her, she laughed.

"You sold us to Theodore James?" He nodded and looked at her with suspicion. "You really are too stupid. When did you do this? Six months ago? It couldn't have been much sooner than that, because the man is dead."

"You lie." He knew that she couldn't lie, especially to him, but he stood over her and screamed at her again. "He said that he'd buy all of the women I could bring him for a price. I would have had one more if you hadn't made me kill your sister Olivia."

"*I* made you kill her? How the hell did you come up with that idea? I tried to hide her away from you, not bring her to your bed like you said." She felt her body beginning to heal and put her hand over the largest wound on her arm. Someone was feeding her.

"You should have made her listen to me. You were her sister. You should have made her do what I wanted and she might not have been murdered." She didn't know what to say to him because she just realized how insane he was. "I had to kill her so that she'd not tell Viktor. He would have gone to Father, and Father would have never given me the kingdom and I wanted it."

"So you killed my sister because she wouldn't let you fuck her, and now in your sick, twisted-up mind, you think to blame me for it?" She snorted at him at the same time she felt someone touch her mind. It was Keith.

We're very close to you. Did you know that you're in another realm? Viktor said that he and his father will have Dakamon subdued in a few minutes. She felt his fear. *Are you hurt, love?*

I'm busted up pretty good but nothing you can't fix for me. She let him feel her body's injuries, and his love settled over her. *The other women are feeding me, aren't they?*

Yes, we all are. Viktor is afraid that they won't be able to make it in time to save you. He seems to think that his brother will try something as soon as he is contacted by his accomplice. She wasn't sure they would make it either. Dakamon had gotten up and was pacing the room as he continued to tell her what she'd done to get him banished from Ravengric.

He stopped suddenly and looked at her. "What have you done? How did you contact my brother and tell him where we are?"

"Magic." He glared at her and she stood up. "I'm not going to tell you but once, Dakamon. You need to step down and come with me quietly. If you don't, I'm going to have to use force."

Harley thought about Mrs. Golden and wondered if she'd ever forgive her if she simply killed this man. She knew that she wouldn't and was saddened by that. The woman had been so nice to her since she'd come to the family, and now this man was going to fuck it all up for her. When Dakamon came toward her with his arms raised, she hesitated for several seconds to see if he would change his mind. But he didn't and she paid for those precious seconds. As his blade sliced through her, she reached out with all the power that was being fed to her and pushed it into his face. As soon as it touched him, he stopped moving and looked at her.

"Dakamon, son of Achard Ravengric, former king of Ravengric, and brother to Viktor Ravengric, I sentence you to death." She dropped to her knees as blood poured from her. "As guardian to the other worlds and realms, I hereby sentence you to die by my hand."

As he dropped to his knees as well, she could see the disbelief on his face. Then the pain. She knew that in a few more seconds he'd be gone, his body disintegrating as if he'd had his head removed. But she'd done more to him than that. She'd given him the light of the sun within his body. And when he exploded, she dropped to the floor and let the darkness take her.

Chapter 13

"I'm so sorry, son, she's dead." Viktor looked at his father as he stood over Harley. "He sliced her throat open and she's bled out. I'm so sorry."

Viktor moved his father out of the way to check for himself. There was no way that she was dead. He felt her pulse, and there wasn't one. He felt his anguish build even as the room filled with the Golden family. He couldn't even speak when Keith asked him if she was all right.

He knew the moment that Keith realized that his true love was gone. He pulled her into his arms and held her as he cried out over and over for her to come back to him. That he needed her more than he did his next breath. When Brock tried to help him, to check on her, he supposed, Viktor looked at the young Rayne, who stood back from them all. She looked as if she was terrified. When she looked at him, he could see her anger as well.

"You did this." She pointed at him. "This is entirely your fault. Had you and your kind stayed in your own realm, none of this would have—"

"He would have come anyway. He would have—" She hit him and Viktor staggered back from the blow. "Rayne, I'm sorry, but he would—"

"I'm not talking about now. I'm talking about all those years ago. All those decades ago you sent her here to die. You knew, all of you knew, that if you sent her here, you were sentencing her to her own death. Why? So you could fulfill some sort of sick fucking joke to your world? So that you could sleep at night, knowing that you helped out the Goldens but only lost one of us? You motherfucker, stand up so that I can hit you again."

Brock moved up to her and tried to calm her, but she tossed him off as well. When she lunged for Viktor, he tried to get away, but she was much faster. And when she shifted he had a moment of panic, when suddenly there was another white tiger standing in front of her. The two of them snarled at him, but finally Rayne backed off.

Peter moved to stand near him and held out his hand. Viktor didn't take it but stared at it. He did feel guilty for Harley's death, but not in the way that Rayne thought he should. He'd told her she'd be safe if they worked together. He'd brought them together because they.... He looked at Peter's hand again.

"Together they can survive." Peter looked at him oddly and Viktor stood up. "Together they can survive."

He moved to Keith, who was still holding Harley. Viktor noticed that her wound, fatal that it was, seemed to be sealing. Looking around the room, he could see them all but Sandra. He looked at Peter.

"Get Sandra. She needs to be here too." He nodded once and disappeared, only to return seconds later with her in his arms. She was as grief-stricken as the family was, and Viktor wondered which one had told her that her daughter-in-law was dead.

"You can heal her." None of them paid him any mind, and he finally had to use his own magic to get them to stop grieving and listen. When they all looked at him, he glanced at Harley. It was working. Even without their touching her, she was healing.

Almost giddy with relief, he looked at Keith. "You all must hold her. She will only survive this if you all hold her. Together you're as strong as you'll ever be. Hold her as a family and you'll save her."

"She's dead." Viktor shook his head at Keith and lifted her chin up so he could see that she was healing. "Oh, Christ," he said as he reached for his family. As they gathered around her and held each other, Viktor felt the power begin to fill the tiny room until the walls seemed to expand with it. When Keith cried out, he knew it had worked and he left them to their reunion. He didn't realize his father and mother had followed him back to Ravengric.

Viktor was still in his room eight days later when there was a sharp knock at his door. He didn't bid them entry because he'd been turning them away for days now and hoped this person would get the hint as well. Apparently not, because the door opened.

Not bothering to turn, he spoke to the person who dared enter his room without his permission. "I've asked to be alone. Is it too much to ask that my request be honored? I'm in mourning."

"You have a visitor, my lord. She is most insistent that you see her." Viktor leaned back in his chair as his servant still stood there. "Sire, what shall I tell her?"

"Tell her that I'm not receiving visitors now, to please come back in a month." Viktor was going to be gone by then, so it mattered little to him if she came back or not. "Tell her that things are not well in the castle, that she'll need to make an appointment."

"Very good, sir." He started to leave but stopped, just turning away. "Sire, would you like for me to send you someone? It has been several days since you have fed, and there is any number of persons that would gladly help you."

"No, tell them I said thanks but not today. I'm not...tell them perhaps tomorrow." He settled back in his chair, only to hear the door open again. "Omar, please don't bother me now. I've come here to—"

"Omar said you refused to see me. I want to know what the hell you're doing in here that you think is so fucking important that you can't come out for ten minutes." He stood and looked at Harley as she stood there, nearly shimmering with anger. "I've not been here in all this time and you are going to send me back without a proper welcome?"

He stared at her for several minutes as the sight of her seemed to pour over him. She was healthy and well was all he could think, and when she took a step toward him, he took one back. He had an idea why she was here, and he might welcome it if he wasn't suddenly so unsure.

"Have you come to finish the job?" She stopped moving, and a long sword appeared in her hand before she started walking again. "I have been expecting you. For days now I've been thinking of what I'd say to you when you came here to kill me."

"And what profound statement have you no doubt come up with? Surely you haven't thought to beg me for forgiveness, have you? Have you a pretty speech that tells me had you not brought the Goldens to me, I'd be dead and not here to do my job?" She didn't look inclined to listen to his answers, so he didn't bother giving her one. "Or did you think to simply let me remove your head from your shoulders as it is written to be?"

"Let you, I believe. I would ask you one thing. Are you happy?" She seemed startled by the question, so he continued. "I know that what happened to you was my fault, but I would like to know that as you bring about my sentence you are somewhat happy."

"I am. Very much so." She pointed the sword down so that the point now rested in the carpet. If his mother could see her, she'd have her head. His mother had made this particular rug when he'd been born. "Why do you think I'm here to behead you, my lord?"

"I am guilty of all the crimes that you have been informed of." He saw her brow rise. "I was brought my letter the second day here. I know of what I've been accused."

"Do you? Apparently you've not read the last page where it says that you're not going to be killed, but made king." He looked at the file that had been left for him days ago that he'd only glanced at. "I see now that you've only done half of what is expected of you. Is that the sort of king you wish to be?"

"I cannot be king, Harley, and we both know it. I have no mate and, as such, am not worthy of the throne. Father will run it until such time that we can elect a new one —" He glared at her. "Why do you shake your head?"

"My sister would be very disappointed in you." He felt the pain of her mentioning Olivia like she'd sliced through his heart. "I don't know what to tell her."

"Tell her?" He sat down hard and felt the tears fill his eyes. "Harley, why are you hurting me this way? Be done with your job so that I may join her in the other life."

"Olivia isn't dead, Viktor." He looked at her and was terrified that she'd been more hurt than he'd realized. "When your brother 'killed' her, he didn't know that in her death I knew. For the three days that everyone thought her dead, I was helping her escape. It was the only way to save her."

His mind tried to work around what she was saying to him when she moved. There stood his love just in the doorway. When she didn't move, Viktor thought it was a trick and turned to Harley.

"This is beyond cruel to me. I know that I have done a great many things to you that bordered on breaking the laws of our kind, but I did them for you, for all of you. To tell me that my Olivia has been alive for all these years and not ever tell me is bad enough. But to bring me a vision of her to torture me is cruel even for —"

"Viktor?" Olivia moved toward him slowly and he held his breath as she spoke again. "I wouldn't allow her to tell you. Had you known, Dakamon would have killed you to keep you from finding out the truth. He wanted you as dead as the others. I never thought he'd do so much to his family for power."

He touched her face when she was only a few inches away from him. Viktor could feel her warmth, but was still afraid to get his hopes up. He realized that Harley was speaking and looked at her.

"I healed her as best I could. There wasn't much time but I knew that if I took her back, even to the infirmary, she'd be dead before the next rising. I had to do something quickly, so I took her to another realm with the hopes of someday going back for her. But I was banished to the human world and knew that Dakamon was keeping tabs on me. Then when you and Peter showed up...I thought Peter was —"

"You thought he was still with Dakamon." She nodded at him. "But later, when you found out. You could have told me then."

"I wouldn't let her. He was so close to you by then that I was...I was afraid for you. For both of you. He'd been so...." Olivia pulled him into her arms. "Oh Viktor, I'm so sorry. I did it for us so that someday we'd have a life together. I love you so very much."

Viktor heard the door close with a quiet click and held his mate until the tears finally stopped flowing down his cheeks. He had his one true love back. After all this time, he had her back. And Viktor decided he was going to live every day showing her how happy he was to have her.

~~~

"I'm leaving in the morning." Keith looked around his house, trying to think what else he might want to take with him, and found another stack of pictures. Ryland was sitting in the chair staring at him as if he had two heads.

"I don't want you to leave." Keith thought that was an understatement but didn't comment to his brother. "Where is Harley? Maybe I can convince her that you need to stay here."

He felt his heart twist as he answered Ryland. "She left yesterday. She had some things to do and thought that if she went to Ravengric early, she could spend my first few days there showing me around."

She'd said that she'd spend it showing him off, but he was still slightly embarrassed about that. They didn't have all that many were-tigers there, but a great many tigers. He stuffed the pictures in with his clothes and sat on the couch. He didn't want to leave either, but he could see where his brother might not understand why Harley felt the need to go.

"Will you be back?" Keith didn't answer him. In truth he was told he could come back, but Harley told him she wouldn't. There was too much here that she didn't want to face.

"Did you know that Viktor's mate was alive?" Ryland looked at him, confused. "Harley had hidden her away so that Dakamon wouldn't kill her. It was Olivia's idea. She thought that if Dakamon found out she was alive he would have beheaded her and that would have been the end of her. Harley took her to see Viktor this morning. It's one of the things she had to do today."

"That must have been a wonderful reunion. I bet Viktor was amazed to have his mate back." Ryland leaned back in his chair. "You didn't answer me. I can only assume that you don't plan on it, and that's not right. Why? What happened that Harley decided to return to Ravengric that you couldn't convince her to stay?"

"I didn't try." Keith stood up and walked to the window. "She won't be back, but she has assured me that I may return as often as I wish. There is a way for you all to come to visit me if you wish as well."

They both looked at the door when it opened and his mom and the others walked in. Keith had hoped to avoid this by only telling Ryland, but apparently he'd taken upon himself to tell them he was leaving anyway. He glared at his oldest brother as the rest of his family filled out the room.

"So she's decided to run with her tail between her legs." Keith looked at Ally as she practically snarled at him. "Of all the cruel heartless things she could do, this really tops the list."

"You don't understand. There are —" Bronwyn cut him off with a snort. "She and I have to have a fresh start. She wants this and I want her to have it."

Keith didn't look at his mom. She was the real reason that Harley wanted to go to Ravengric to live. And no matter how much he tried to convince her otherwise, she felt as if his mom would never forgive her for killing Dakamon without a trial. He looked out the window and tried to wrap his mind around the fact that he wasn't going to see his family again. Harley had told him several times, hundreds of times, that he could come back daily if he wanted, but he didn't want to leave her. And he wouldn't.

"I'm sorry." He looked around at his mom, who stood just behind him. The others had gone and he hadn't even realized it.

"For what?" He looked out the window again instead of at her, afraid she'd see the truth. But she brought his chin around to face her, and he could see she was hurt too. "She's not coming back here."

"Because of me." He didn't answer her, not sure if he could. "I knew as soon as Ryland told me that you were packing up that it was because of me. I said that to her and now she'll take…she'll not let me tell her I was wrong."

"I don't know that she thinks you were wrong. Harley has nightmares almost nightly because of what she did to Dakamon. Killing him was…she knew that it was him or her. And since she thought she was dying anyway, she didn't want to take the chance of him coming back for the rest of us."

"She thought of me before she blacked out." Harley had told him that as well, but not that his mom had known. "I felt it. She wondered if I'd forgive her for this, and I felt her hurt from me. I've never…when she was resting here, I thought to come and see her about it, but I never…I just couldn't do it, I was so ashamed. Then when Ryland said she was gone, I knew I'd…I don't want either of you to go. Not like this."

"She's afraid you'll not forgive her." Keith moved to his things to finish packing them up as he continued. "I don't know if I'll be back soon, but I'll try. She said it's a simple matter of moving between the realms and I'll come back soon."

"No, you won't." He looked at his mom. "I have a feeling she told you that you could, but you have no intentions of leaving her. Not that I can blame you. She is your mate, but she won't come, so you won't. I understand, but I don't have to like it."

Keith sat down again, his heart crushing under the weight of all this. He felt Harley touch his mind and she sent him her love. He smiled sadly at Sandra, knowing that she was hurting too, but she was putting up such a brave front.

"She told me that she loved you dearly and couldn't stand to see the look of disappointment or shame in your face. When you didn't come and see her, she felt…she said she knew that things were never going to be right between you, and she didn't think she could stand it. Not now."

"Why not now?" Keith looked at his mom and then away. "Keith Golden, you tell me right now, or so help me I will take you to the wood shed and beat you within an inch of your life."

"We're having a baby." He got up to pace. "She didn't want you to treat our child differently than you did the other grandchildren, and she knew that you would. I tried to tell her that you loved her, but she said that you might at that, but you'd never respect her after this thing with Dakamon. I told her that she'd had no choice in the matter, that it was her or him and you'd be happy with the end results. But she's set on this."

His mom sat down in the chair he'd just gotten up from. He could feel her pain. Hell, he had his own in all this, but he loved Harley and he'd never do anything to hurt her. Not ever again. When she'd left him yesterday to go to Ravengric, she'd cried the entire time, even knowing that they'd be together in a few short days.

"Take me to her." Keith looked at his mom, not sure he'd heard her correctly. "I want you to take me to her right this minute. I'll not have her thinking I'm ashamed of her for one more minute. You take me to her, or so help me I'll figure out a way myself and get there. Of all the…what on earth was she thinking, taking my grandchild away from me? Well? Are we going?"

"I can't. I mean I can, but I can't take you there without permission. Until I'm made a citizen of the realm, I can only go back and forth on my own." He tried to think how to get his mom there, because she wasn't looking any happier at him with every second that passed. "I can call Viktor…no, that won't work. He's with his mate. I suppose I could—"

"His mate? I thought Viktor's mate was dead?" His mom tapped her foot. "That girl has a great deal of explaining to do and when I find her, I do hope there is a willow tree nearby. I'm going to need the entire tree before this is finished."

"Perhaps I can be of assistance." Achard appeared in the room just as Keith was about to confess he had no idea how to get his mom there. "You'll only need to close your eyes, Lady Golden, and I'll have us all there in a few moments. My wife wishes to meet with you first, if you don't mind. Come along, Lord Keith, we have a journey to make."

Before he could grab up his bags, he was standing in an antechamber filled with flowers and Achard's mate Parthinia. Tea was being served just as they entered the room. There was something very odd about her smile, and he was almost afraid to find out what it meant.

"I've had Harley arrested. I'm not sure she's very happy with me at the moment, but she'll get over it. I do hope you can convince her to come back to your realm with you, my dear. I would certainly hate to have to have her beheaded after all of this."

Chapter 14

"Let me the fuck out of here." Harley was no longer yelling, but she was still pissed off. Yelling hadn't gotten her anything but a sore throat, because she was pretty sure she was the only one listening anyway. When she heard a noise, she didn't even bother looking. The guard that was there had told her in no uncertain terms he was not going to let her out.

"You've gotten yourself in a pickle now, haven't you?" Harley looked at Sandra, then resumed her pacing. "Do sit down. I don't wish to watch you burn off your anger about something you should have known was going to get you into trouble. What did you think was going to happen to you when you brought out a dead woman after thousands of years? A welcoming party?"

"I didn't think beyond reuniting my sister with her mate." She hadn't meant to answer her, but she did continue her pacing. "What is it you want? Come to tell me you thought I'd end up here? You should be happy. Once I'm gone, Keith will be free to do what he pleases."

"And the baby you carry, what will happen to it once your head is not on your shoulders?"

Harley stumbled a little in her pace but didn't stop. "So he told you, did he? No matter. They'll simply wait for me to birth him. Then they'll do what needs to be done." She rubbed her hand over the smoothness of her belly. "I would imagine that should make you happy."

"Why would you think that?"

Harley made a turn at the end of her cell and wiped at the tears before answering Sandra.

"There won't be someone there to influence your grandson into making choices that don't line up with what you think of as right." Sandra snorted at her, and Harley stopped moving to stare at her. "You'd help him raise my son, wouldn't you? You'd not hold what I did against him, would you?"

"And what is it you think you've done that I would wish you dead for? Killing a man who was bent on killing my family? And that does include you, young lady. Take out a monster that killed thousands of women over his lifetime, not to mention his own brothers? Did you know that he had plans to kill off his father, as well as Viktor?"

"Yes. His mother, too, I would guess, but he never thought of her much beyond being the one who brought him into this world, as was her duty." Harley sat on the small cot that had been unused until then. "What do you want, Sandra? Did you come to make sure that I'm really a prisoner? I assure you I am."

"I suppose I deserve most of how you feel about me, but not all." Sandra looked at her hard before she continued. "Or is it you hope that you'll piss me off enough that I'll convince Keith he's better off without you and take him home with me? Not going to happen, I'm happy to say. In fact, Alistair is working on a trial for you, and the others are working on an appeal. There are a great many Goldens in your corner right now, including me."

Harley was surprised by that. But then the Goldens were nothing if not surprising. She looked around the tiny cell she'd been brought to two days ago. There was the cot with a thick mattress on it, as well as a sink and toilet. She had a curtain that she could pull over the door and a window that was about ten feet off the ground. It was very different from the rooms she'd been staying in here waiting for Keith to come back, and much different than the house that belonged to him. She wondered if he'd live there after she was—

"Are you going to answer me?" Harley didn't have a clue what she'd been saying and told her. "I asked you if you would consider coming back to our realm and living out your life with Keith and the rest of us. The king and queen said that it would be all right with them so long as you knew that coming here again would mean your death."

"I'm not sure I believe it could be that easy." She didn't want to, as a matter of fact. "I have family here, too...my sister and Viktor. Not to mention I have a little family left there as well. Not like you do, but some."

"They are welcome to come to us. Even stay with us for as long as they want." Her voice sounded hopeful, but Harley wasn't fooled. "Harley, I'm so sorry for what I said to you. I was wrong on so many levels that I can never tell you how sorry I am."

"He had to die." Sandra nodded. "I mean, he had to die by my hand. None of the others could have...they would have been able to kill him, but they never would have survived. I couldn't let them die, not like—"

"Not like you did." Harley shrugged, not sure sometimes that she should have lived. "I was there when they saved you. I had to be. When you were nearly dead, they were working so hard to save you but it wasn't working. They came for me, and my touch, my love for you, brought you back too. And I do love you, Harley Golden. With all my heart."

"I can't be what you want me to be. I'm not like the others. I'm hard and a loner. I've been around a great deal longer than all of them, and I've seen things, done things that would make you more ashamed than you were before."

"I was ashamed at me, not you, and all of them have done things they are not proud of. Even my sons haven't been saints. And I'm sure as the years go on, you'll see that Keith has his faults too. Even though he is my baby, he's not perfect."

"I know that. It's why I love him." Harley put her hand on her belly again. "I'm going to have a son. Keith doesn't know it yet, but it's a boy. My kind...we can tell from the moment of conception what the child will be, and he'll be tiger first and all our magic second. He'll be what we never were."

"He'll be loved, and that's what the most important thing is." A chair was brought for Sandra, and she thanked the guard who'd brought it to her. He winked at her, and Harley wanted to scream at him for ignoring her for all this time. "Why have you been arrested? Do you know?"

"I don't know really. I'm assuming now it was so that they could go and bring you here. I wouldn't put it past them." She leaned back against the wall, putting her feet up on the mattress to watch her. "Did you know that this world was created to harbor beings without homes? When Achard and Parthinia created this realm, they came here with only three others. One was Peter. Peter had grand ideas that they could keep out humans, who had murdered his entire family, and make it a safe place for any and all who wanted to live out their days without fear."

"You came as well." Harley nodded. "How old are you? I know it's rude to ask a woman that, but you look to be in your mid-twenties. I'm assuming you're a good deal older than that."

"Three thousand four hundred and twelve on my last birthday. I'm nearly a thousand years older than Peter, and older than both the king and queen by almost that much. Maven is older than me by nearly five hundred years. She's not as nice as me though." Sandra burst out laughing, and Harley joined her. "I can be nice. I just don't like to be."

"You're very sweet and I love you." Sandra stared at her for several minutes, and Harley let her. She had little to hide from her and would tell her whatever it was she was thinking about asking her. "Will Keith live longer than his family?"

"No." Sandra nodded, then looked away until she said her name. "You all will live a great deal longer than you would have before I came into your lives. Not by decades, but by thousands of decades times thousands. You're immortal. Just as I am. The only way to end your lives now is to have your head removed from your body. And only then can it be done by the king or queen of this realm. We are all Ravengrics now. All of us."

"The children, too, as will their children and their children?" Harley nodded. "I see. And what will we do in all these years as a family? Will we have normal lives?"

"I would suppose you'd be able to do whatever you wanted. As for normal? I'm not sure what normal is. I'm sure you don't either. Nor do most people, I would guess. I will tell you this...you have a mate out there. He'll not be like Keith's father, but more. He'll take good care of you, keep you happy, and he'll give you a daughter, though not by your body."

"I don't want a mate. I loved once. That's all I need or want." Harley didn't say anything, knowing that she'd already met him and they had already touched. When the guard came down the hall again, he had a small table and set it near Sandra, with a plate of cookies and a cup of tea on top. Sandra was thinking too hard to notice, but she did thank him. Harley wanted to laugh. It was beginning.

"What will I say to him? What...will I know him when I see him?" Harley looked down the hall again before answering her.

"Apparently not."

~~~

When she walked around the room again, Ryland nearly told her to sit down, but Bronwyn told him to wait. Harley had been in his office for nearly an hour, and still she'd not said one word other than to say *yes* when he'd asked her if Keith knew she was here.

I have things to do rather than watch her touch all my things in this office. I'm pretty sure she can look at them without us sitting here. Bronwyn told him to behave. *Did you know that the mayor wants me to run for office? I don't have time for that either. I have a family to keep in line.*

And you do that so well. Perhaps you should think of taking the job. It might get you out among the living for a while, and it'll certainly keep me from killing you. She glared at him when he told her he wasn't doing anything. *Ryland, you told me this morning that I was making the bed incorrectly, that it needed to have the sheets measured to assure it was even on the bed. You need to get out.*

He'd been lonely and she'd been in the bedroom with Gabby. His daughter thought it was funny when he got out the ruler. And now that he thought about it, she'd been laughing pretty hard when her mother had hit him with the pillows. Where had Bronwyn's sense of humor gone?

Out the door when you decided to work from home all the time. What would it take for you to leave me to some peace for a few hours daily? He had a thought, and she shut him down. *We can't have sex all the time. Gabby requires some of my attention.*

"Keith and I are having a baby. A boy." They both looked at Harley when she finally spoke. "He'll be born in late November."

She was staring out the window near the fireplace, and more than likely didn't see the exchange between him and Bronwyn. He was shocked and, apparently, so was his mate.

"I hadn't known. Are you well?" Harley nodded at Bronwyn without turning. "I bet Keith is happy. We've not had a boy born in this family yet."

"You're going to have a son as well. So will the rest of the women when they next breed." She turned to them then. "Would you like to know more about them? I can tell you. Anything you want, including who their mates will be."

She sounded bitter and Ryland wasn't sure what to say to her. When she moved from the window to the wall of books, she took one down and handed it to Bronwyn. She looked at the cover and then handed it to him. It was the book that he'd gotten from his mother when his father had died.

"I saw him. Your father. He was there when...when I died. He shoved me back here and gave me a message to give to the two of you." Harley started pacing and stopped near a picture of his family with their dad in the middle. Ryland thought his mom had taken it, which would explain why she wasn't in it.

"Why...my father died a long time ago, Harley. Are you telling me that you saw him in the afterlife?" She nodded, then shook her head. Before he could ask her which, Bronwyn spoke.

"You saw him when you died and he told you it wasn't your time yet. I'm guessing that has you a little on edge. Tell us what he said." Harley looked at Bronwyn, then at him. He saw her smile, but it was one that said you're so not going to like this.

"He said to tell you to expand your horizons and move on. There are over nine thousand cats in the world that are without support and leadership, and you're sitting on your ass not doing a damned thing to help them." He started to tell her that she was wrong when she continued. "He said that you are to take the Goldens to the Olympics and win him some gold. He had me repeat that five times to him to make sure I said it correctly."

Ryland felt the blood drain from his face and he had to put his head on the desk. He heard Bronwyn say his name, but he was having a little trouble breathing right now. When he lifted his head, he looked right at Harley.

"Did he tell you how I was supposed to do this?" She nodded. "And I suppose this is going to make you some sort of helper to me. Someone I'm going to need to make this happen."

"I have money." He nodded, knowing that she had money but not sure what that had to do with things. "And property. All of Dakamon's came to me, as well as his riches. It's the way I'm paid as a guardian. And Achard has given me my 'back wages,' I think he called them."

"I don't know...congratulations, I suppose, but what does that have to do with me bringing my father gold? And so you know, he said that to us every time we had a test of life. He didn't tell us what to do, but said that whatever would bring good things to our name was golden to him."

"How will you house this many people, and where will you put them once they get here? And by the way, they'll start coming soon. Tomorrow as a matter of fact. They won't expect you to keep them all, but to help them set up streaks across the world for them. Your brothers are going to be leaders like you." He shook his head and she nodded. "They will be. And you knew this all along. It's what your father wanted."

"He said we'd be great men among the masses. He never said we'd be separated." Ryland shook his head again. "I won't have my family separated again. I love having them here."

Harley moved toward him, touching things as she went. A book that had been left out, a lamp that was his father's, and a blanket that he'd wrapped Gabby in last night when she'd wanted him to read to her. All the things disappeared when Harley put her hands on his desk.

"All these things have meaning to you, don't they?" He nodded. "Then bring them to you." He looked at her oddly and thought of the items. Each one appeared just where it had been. "Your brothers are just as meaningful to you. Bring them to you. Careful of Alistair and Ally, they are...busy."

Keith appeared first, and he was drinking a glass of tea. He was still in his pajamas and had no shirt on. He set down the glass and reached for Harley, who went to his arms willingly. Next he brought Jules, who was dressed in his work clothes that were covered in clay. He had a small ball of clay in his hands when he glared.

"You could have simply said something first." Jules tore off a piece of the clay he had in his hands and threw it at his brother. Ryland dodged it but not the second one. He was still laughing when his mother walked in the room. She looked around at them all and sat down.

"You've told him then." Harley nodded at her and sat down. "You should know that I believe her. And I agree with your father. Get up off your ass and let's get this taken care of."

"I'm not even sure where to begin." Keith handed him a thick file, and he opened it to the first page. There was a picture of a man who'd lost an eye, and he looked like someone had beaten him pretty badly.

"Dan Copper, age fifty-four. His cat was injured when he was trapped by some humans and he couldn't shift to help him heal. As a result he lost his eye and was shunned from the streak he was with. Nine days ago he tried to kill himself. This morning I went to see him, and he's going to be coming here when he's released from the hospital. The next person is Eli Wayne. He's twenty-two and has never been in a streak before. He was changed by his girlfriend, who was killed three days later when her father found out about Eli. He's been on the run since. He'll be coming today and will be staying with us until he can get himself a job."

The list went on and on, and before they'd gotten halfway through this file, Alistair and Ally came with another one, this one thicker. By the time they had started listing the people, hanging names up on a long wipe-off board that Brock brought in, each of the brothers knew where they were headed. Keith and Harley were going to stay here until things were set up at each of the new streaks. His mother was crying when they sat down to dinner.

"I thought I'd be okay with this. Knowing that your father was going to get his wish and see his sons be great leaders." Ryland held her as she sobbed. "I know I'm being a silly old woman, aren't I?"

"No. I'm going to miss them as well." Ryland looked around the dining room that had been added onto over the years. "We're a hell of a family, aren't we? And as you know, we're going to come here once a week to be a family with you. All of us, and you can visit them whenever you want."

As dinner progressed and got louder as they passed around food, Ryland had a moment when he missed his dad. He would have loved this, been in the middle of all the conversations as well as the butt of a great many of the jokes. Ryland glanced at his brothers with their mates and curled his hand into Bronwyn's. This was what life was about. Food, family, and laughter. He reached for Gabby when she toddled toward him.

"Daddy, where is my dolly?" He reached under the table and handed it to her. She cuddled it into her neck and smiled at him. "I'm going to be a great leader someday too. Aunt Harley told me that I can be whatever I want. She said I could be a princess, too, but said I should hold out for better pay. What does that mean?"

Ryland looked at Harley as Keith put his hand over her belly. "It means you can be whatever you want, like she said, but to make sure it's what you want, not what you settle for."

He was sure she still didn't understand, but she would someday, and now thanks to Harley, he'd be around to see that she would. As the table started to be cleared, he reached for Harley's hand and pulled her to him for a hug.

"You're fucking with your brother, aren't you?" He laughed, then hugged her tighter when Keith growled. "You do know that we're going to have amazing sex because of this, right?"

He pushed her away from him so quickly that she stumbled. She was laughing so hard at him that he wanted to grab her again and mark her, but Bronwyn stepped between them. She looked up at him as she cradled Gabby in her arms.

"If you behave yourself, I'll let you use that nice feather on me again. I have to put Gabby to bed, but that should only take about ten minutes." His cock hardened at the thought of Bronwyn tied to his bed and him using that wonderful peacock feather on her again. Nodding, he followed her up after the rest of his family left. He thought about what else Harley had told him.

"You'll need to make sure that Peter has a part in what we're doing. He's still mad at me for locking him and Maven in the cell." Ryland wondered how that was going for the vampire and laughed. "He's going to be well and truly mated when you see him again."

Chapter 15

Peter glanced around the room again. He'd been here for eleven days, and he was either going to have to be let out soon or he was going to have to murder Maven. She was driving him crazy, and he thought she knew it. When she stretched again, pulling her arms over her head, he whimpered. Christ, he wasn't going to be able to keep his distance much longer.

"You know I can feel your need, right?" He stepped closer to the wall to try and pull the darkness around him. Harley had taken his magic as well as his ability to contact anyone when she'd put him here with Maven. He was going to strangle her when he was released.

"I don't know what you're talking about." Peter backed up more when Maven came toward him. He'd had the feeling for the last two days that she was going to try something, and he was prepared for her. Or so he thought. When she took off her blouse, he felt his mouth water.

"It's warm in here, don't you think?" And getting hotter, he wanted to tell her, but was afraid to open his mouth. When she unhooked her bra, he watched, mesmerized, while she left it there and it cupped her breasts like her skin. When she lifted her arms up again, Peter felt his fangs drop with need.

"Do you know what you're doing? Of course you do. You think you're going to be able to make me mate with you, but I won't do it. I refuse to have your father pissed at me because you have an itch." She laughed, and even that was sexy to him. "Maven, put your clothes back on. Please?"

Her pants were off before he could say anything, and she stood before him in her open bra and panties. Peter tried to close his eyes to the beauty before him, but they refused to do as he wanted. When she touched his chest, all the air he'd been holding in his lungs seemed to hiss from him.

"Don't you want to drink from me, Peter?" He caught himself nodding and stopped. "I have just what you need. Warm blood just waiting for you to drink from me."

"I won't do it." He put his hands on her hips to push her away from him, only to find her flush against his body. "You're playing with fire, Maven. Once I bite you, I won't stop at that."

"Good." She moaned when he rocked into her juncture. "More please, Peter. I want to feel you drink from me."

He turned her around, knowing that this was going to end badly. When she wrapped her arms around his shoulders, he took her mouth as gently as he could, but the moment he touched her, hunger seemed to take him. He ate at her mouth, tasting her sweetness.

When he lifted her up, her legs wrapping around his hips, he knew that he was finished. She was his, and he had to have her. Lifting his head from her mouth, he looked at her eyes and could see her hunger too. But he had to make sure.

"You'll be my mate." She nodded. "I won't have you saying that I took from you without permission."

"I won't. Please, take me, Peter. I've waited my whole life for you." He licked the pounding pulse at her throat and tasted her essence. There was no way he could turn back now even if his life depended on it. Peter willed his clothes away as he nipped at her flesh.

His body ached now. He had to have her, needed her with a passion as old as he was and a need as great as he'd ever had. When she rocked her body to his, he felt her slickness as she rode his cock, and he adjusted her so that he was just at her entrance. Lifting his head again, he looked into her eyes as he pulled her over him. Christ, it was like having a torch touching him.

Filling her had never felt like this with any other woman. Her sheath was tight, and he felt her milk him even as he buried himself to the root. When he was as deep as he could get, he held her still.

"I'm going to mark you and when I do, you will bite me as well." She nodded and her sheath gripped him. "Maven, if you keep that up, I won't be able to see to your pleasure before mine."

"Peter, the moment you sink your teeth into me, I'm going to come so hard that you'll have to hang on to me." Proving her point, she rolled her hips and moaned. "I can't wait for you much longer. Please, Peter, take me."

He couldn't wait. The second he moved, rocked into her, he knew that he was going to come soon. When he licked her throat again, nipping at the tender flesh there, he felt her tighten around him. The moment he sank his fangs deep into her vein, she screamed out his name and he did hold her. Christ, he thought as his own release flooded her, he should have done this a long time ago.

Their climax was hard, and it took his breath away. When she came again, digging her nails into his back, he sealed the wound at her throat and took her mouth. The connection was there, and he had to slow down her emotions as she flooded him with her love. Peter never thought that having someone love him as profoundly as she did could feel so wonderful.

"I want to taste you." She nodded, her body still reacting to her release. When he sat her on the floor, he had to hold her while she steadied. Dropping to his knees, he kissed her hip and made his way to her heat. He looked up at her when she moaned.

"You're beautiful. And all mine." She nodded at him, her fingers curled into his hair as she pulled him to her. "Greedy now, are you?"

"Yes. I need to feel your tongue inside of me. Feel you drink from me while I come. I've thought of nothing else since I was shut away in here with you but to have you. Peter, don't make me wait much longer. I need — " He pulled her clit into his mouth and nipped hard.

She screamed. He sucked harder on her clit and felt her knees tremble and her pussy drench him. Pulling her away from the wall, he guided her to the floor. He wasn't finished yet and if she fell, she might be hurt. As soon as her back touched the floor he went back to eating her and brought her to several more releases until she begged him to stop. Leaning over her, he fisted his cock and watched her face to see if he hurt her as he slowly entered her.

As soon as he was deep, he settled his body over hers and held still. He wanted to pound into her hard and mark her again, but he wanted to enjoy her a bit more. When she wrapped her legs around his waist, he moved gently into her and rocked back and forth while he suckled at one nipple, then the other until she was begging him again. When he slammed deep, she cried out. Peter took her throat the moment she came, shouting out his name. Tearing his mark into her throat, he roared out his own release. She was his. He dropped his weight onto her and lay there as sated as he'd ever been...no, he'd never been this sated in all his life.

"I'm sending Harley a dozen red roses." He laughed when she giggled. "I guess she knew that we'd either kill each other or become mates. For a while there I was worried I'd be a dead man."

"I wouldn't have let you go that long." She shifted under him and he rolled to his back, taking her with him. "You should know that I think Daddy had something to do with this too. He and Harley were talking last week, and I think he arranged this."

"I thought your dad hated me." She shook her head. "He told me to stay away from you or he'd kill me. I think that's about as hate filled as you can get."

"I think he was telling you that so we'd come together. Sort of telling you one thing and hoping for the other. Mother and Daddy have been hinting about grandchildren for months now. I guess when I was bitten by the other vamp, he saw an opportunity and took it." She lifted her head and looked down at him. "Are you mad at him?"

"No. Perhaps I'll send him a dozen roses as well." She snuggled down on his chest. "I wonder how they'll know to let us out."

She lifted her head and looked down at him. "You want to leave here now? I thought...I don't know, I thought we'd use this time to get to know one another."

He rolled her to her back again, wishing they were on the bed when suddenly they were. His magic was back, or someone was helping him. When he reached for Harley, she told him to have fun and when he wanted out, the key was under the footboard. He took Maven's nipple into his mouth as he thanked her. There was no way he was going to leave here before he knew his new mate very, very well.

~~~

Harley tried to concentrate on what Keith was telling her about the computer, but he smelled so good all she wanted to do was to toss him to the desk they were using and have her way with him. When he brushed up against her breast, again showing her how to use the mouse, she'd had enough. Turning to look at him, she cupped his cock in her palm. He stood very still.

"I think we need a break, don't you?" He nodded. "Why don't you take off your pants for me and let me have your cock? I'm sure that once I have you down my throat, I'll be able to think better."

"You haven't been paying much attention anyway." He leaned on the desk in front of her as he opened his pants. His cock thickened in his hand as he fisted himself. "Do you think I could have the chair and you lying back on the desk while I feast from you first?"

"No. I want to suck you until you come." She adjusted the chair so that she was between his legs and licked him from root to crown and moaned. "You have such a wonderful taste. I could do this all day."

"I won't last five minutes if you do that again." She nipped at the vein running hotly along his shaft, and he moaned. "You're going to make me come before you get me into your mouth."

"Then you'll have to come again." She licked his length again and moved her hand to his balls. Rolling them gently, she suckled one into her mouth and rolled her tongue over it. He rocked into her mouth hard, and she knew he was close.

"Baby, take me or let me fuck you. I need to come and I'd rather not come on you but in you." She took off her blouse and bra and tossed them away. Leaning back in the chair, she played with her nipples while he watched. She was sliding her hand down to her pussy when he grabbed her hand.

"What are you doing?" She smiled at him, and using her other hand, slid her fingers into her pussy and moaned. "Let me taste your juices."

She lifted her fingers to his mouth, and he suckled them clean. When she went back to what she was doing, he stood up and moved to the side of the chair, and she took him into her mouth. He started fucking her as she played with her clit.

"Come for me. I want to see you make yourself come while I fuck your mouth." She moved her fingers in and out of her quicker as he watched. "Christ, you're going to kill me."

When she swallowed his cock down her throat, he cried out, and she felt his finger join hers. When he pinched her clit, she screamed around his cock just as his first stream of cum filled her mouth. Over and over he fucked her this way until he jerked from her and put her over the desk, her ass hanging over the edge. He stepped back, and she started to ask him what when he suddenly shifted.

He wants to drink from you. I can't hold him back any longer. She opened her legs for him as his big head came toward her. *Baby, I'm so sorry about this. He just wants a taste.*

His tongue licked her from gate to clit. The roughness of his tongue made her scream out a hard, quick release, but he didn't stop. The more he drank, his tongue filling her the more, she came, harder and harder until she was weak with it. Keith took his cock and filled her so quickly that it took her breath away.

"Come for me. I have to mark you. Come for me now and I'll take your throat." As soon as he started pounding into her, she felt her climax racing over her. When she felt the earth still—everything paused for several seconds—she bowed up off the desk and screamed. The climax was like nothing she'd ever felt before. And when he bit her throat, she came again, feeling the darkness take her over the edge and beyond. There was no way she could survive if he did this to her daily.

She was alone in the bed when she woke. Reaching out to the house, she found him in the office and he wasn't alone. Harley found the shirt she'd had on earlier folded at the foot of the bed, along with a pair of his boxers. She was going to have to get some clothes of her own soon. She couldn't keep wearing his. When she knocked on the door, she went in to find a man with several racks of clothing and dresses and shirts everywhere.

"I was going to surprise you. I should have known better." Keith kissed her on the mouth. "I was putting you to bed when I realized that you've been wearing nothing but my things since you've moved in. I wanted you to feel like you could go out without looking like a homeless person."

"I love wearing your things." He nodded and asked the man to give them a moment. When he stepped out, Keith pulled her into his arms.

"I'm sorry about what my cat did. It didn't bother you, did it?" She shook her head. "Good. I think he wants to do it a great deal more. I've never known him to be so relaxed before."

"Me neither." She picked up one of the dresses and looked at him. "You going to wear this? Because I'm not."

The dress was bright green and short enough that she was sure her butt would hang out if she moved. When he took it from her and pressed it to her body, she could feel his desire. She would wear it now even if it was to see that look on his face again.

"I thought it would be nice to wear when I want to take you out. Then take you once I got you there." She responded to his words and leaned into him. "Behave. We have company. My mom is coming over too. She said something about taking you to the new house."

He had sold this house and was looking for another one. Ryland had bought it from him without quibbling about the price. When Keith swatted her ass, she turned to look at him.

"What will the new house be called?" It was something he'd beaten into her yesterday when she'd mentioned his new house.

"Our house. She's going to go with me to the new house that belongs to us." She glared at him. "I don't know how it's my house when all I've done is just look at pictures. What the hell do we need a house for anyway?"

"Because I don't want my grandson living in a box, thank you very much." Sandra walked into the room the same way she did everything....like it was a command and she wanted things to go her way. Harley loved getting her riled up.

"I don't know what's wrong with a box. I lived in one for many, many years and I turned out okay." She moved past her to the one of the racks of jeans. "Besides, I think that we'd save a great deal of money if we didn't have to heat a house this big and maybe have sex all the time to keep us warm. Keith and I, not the baby."

"Why you wouldn't...what is wrong with you? You can't talk to me like...Harley Golden, you are by far the most infuriating woman I've ever met." Harley raised her brow. "Okay, one of the most infuriating women I've ever met. But only because the others haven't had as much practice as you've had."

"And they won't, either." She sat down suddenly when she felt a wave of dizziness roll over her. That had been happening a great deal lately, and she looked up when Keith handed her a glass of tea. She hated tea normally, but lately it had made her feel better.

"Peter said it's a reaction from being pregnant and the baby not getting enough of whatever it needs," Keith explained to his mom while he massaged her back. "He said she needs to drink more and to try and use less magic. It drains them both."

He winked at her when she looked up at him. His mom had caught the reference right away. "Both? Both her and the baby, you mean?"

Keith shook his head. "We're having twins. Boys. We just figured it out yesterday." Harley watched Sandra, and when she slid into the chair nearest her, she sent Keith to her. She was looking at her like she'd never seen him before.

"Identical?" Harley nodded. "Good heavens, two just like you. Whatever will we do with them?" Harley started to tell her nothing at all when she smiled at her. "Twin boys for me to love and hold. I'm so excited for you both and for me. The others will be so surprised as well. Oh Keith, I'm so glad."

She and Sandra were at the house when she felt a being touch her mind. She tried to ignore it, but they were just too insistent. When she answered them, she felt a smile touch her face.

We're having a baby. I just figured it out. Viktor and I are having a baby and we couldn't be happier. Harley told Sandra, who laughed too. *Oh my God, I'm going to be a mother. A real mother.*

That's what happens when you have a baby, dork. You become a mom. What are you having, and have you told anyone else? She told her a girl and no. "I think Peter and Maven will be making an announcement soon too. The way they've been going at it, it's small wonder they can walk."

Olivia laughed and told her she missed her. *I'll come there soon. Viktor wants to talk to you and Keith about setting up a home for us there so we can get away when we want. You could do that for us, couldn't you?*

Of course. We're looking at houses now. Keith is doing some business with Ryland right now, but I'll tell him later. I'm so happy for you. Tell Viktor I said congrats.

She closed the connection and looked at Sandra, who was staring at her. When she asked her what, the older woman shook her head. "I was just thinking about my son and how happy you've made him. It's hard to believe that not so long ago you were saving his life. Now...now you're having his child and looking at houses with him. I wanted to tell you...I need to tell you how much I love you. All of the other girls too, but you...you've given us so much more than we could ever have had. You've given us love and happiness."

"I didn't do anything but pull a piece of glass out of a man's chest while his brother screamed at me." Sandra laughed when she did. "I love you as well, Sandra. More than I thought I could love. And Keith has made it so easy to love him. He's made me happy as well."

"Good, I'm glad we have that taken care of. Now, I wanted to ask you about that guard, the one that was so nice to me. Did you know that he has a daughter about Ryland's age? And she's so wonderful. She's coming for dinner tomorrow night."

Harley smiled, knowing that Sandra was going to love the extra grandchildren she was going to get when she and Bartholomew married, as well a daughter when she adopted Sarah. As she talked on, Harley put her hand on her small bump and told her sons they were going to be in a loving and generous family when they came. They assured her that they had already figured that out.

About the Author

Kathi Barton, author of the bestselling series Force of Nature, lives in Nashport, Ohio with her husband Paul. In addition to writing full time Kathi likes to spend time with her eight grandkids, three children and three children-in-laws. She writes to relax and have fun.

Her muse, a cross between Jimmy Stewart and Hugh Jackman brings them to life for her readers in a way that has them coming back time and again for more. Her favorite genre is paranormal romance with a great deal of spice. You can visit Kathi on line and drop her an email if you'd like. She loves hearing from her fans. aaronskiss@gmail.com.

Follow Kathi on her blog: http://kathisbartonauthor.blogspot.com/